Harry Feels The Heat!

The flames seemed to roar out of the window in anger after Harry as he plummeted sixteen feet to a side incline. He slammed against that, rolled down, hit another inclined roof right below that, and fell into a pile of sand that had collected against the side of the house. Harry didn't know the extent of his injuries, but he did know he wasn't dead.

Hands plucked at him. They rolled him over. Harry saw figures in blue and yellow uniforms. The cavalry had arrived. He was carried out to the safety of some ambulances across the street. He felt tired. He didn't feel good. The last thing he saw that day was the face of Captain Avery looking down at him with concern.

Harry laughed himself into unconsciousness. . . .

Books by Dane Hartman

Dirty Harry #1: Duel For Cannons

Dirty Harry #2: Death on the Docks

Dirty Harry #3: The Long Death

Published by
WARNER BOOKS

DIRTY HARRY #3

The Long Death

Dane Hartman

WARNER BOOKS

A Warner Communications Company

WARNER BOOKS EDITION

Copyright © 1981 by Warner Books, Inc.
All rights reserved.

Warner Books, Inc., 75 Rockefeller Plaza, New York, N.Y. 10019

A Warner Communications Company

Printed in the United States of America

First Printing: December, 1981

10 9 8 7 6 5 4 3 2 1

Dedication

To Robert Bishop, who doesn't have to draw a picture to really know the ropes.

Acknowledgments

Ed Breslin
Art Bourgeau of the Whodunit Bookstore, Philadelphia, Pa.
Mitch Schultz of Hansen & Company Gunsmiths, Southport, Ct.
The Zen Oriental Book Store, West 57th Street, New York, N.Y.

DIRTY HARRY #3

The Long Death

"Time to air out a bit."

Chapter One

She had always been proud of her feet. Many beautiful girls had reason to be pleased with their bright eyes, their aristocratic noses, their full lips, their handsome lungs, their smooth ivory hips, their long legs, or their lustrous hair, but Barbara had been proudest of her feet. She had been proud because quite often it was the feet that threw been
off the perfection of an otherwise gorgeous girl.

As curvaceous and striking as a girl might think herself, very few appreciated their feet. Either there were too many veins along the top or their soles were too rough or their nails weren't right or, as in most cases, the toes would have the wrong symmetry. Either the second toe was longer than the big toe or the middle toes were too bumpy or the little toe was all scrunched up.

Not Barbara though. Barbara's feet had been perfect. They were small, delicately shaped, and the toes lined up like the King Family children—all blond, pearly, and in perfectly diminishing height. Barbara had rarely been more excited than when she placed her terrific feet into a pair of strong hands for a massage. She hadn't done it for

9

a while, of course. There were very few strong hands she would trust with her feet at the University of California at Berkeley. It seemed as if all the summer courses were being taken by either wimps or fairies. All the good hands were sunning themselves at the beach.

Barbara had promised herself and her feet a little sojourn by the bay. She had told herself that the very next weekend would be spent socializing. There was no reason she'd have to bury her pert little nose in the books all the time. She would pack her tight, sleek form into a bright maillot and do a little advertising, she decided. Yes, the very next weekend

But now it was too late.

Her feet were slashed and bleeding. Their shapely form was warped by swelling. Each tortured step marked a lightning rod of pain up both her slim legs. Her feet were not the only things she had been proud of, and they were not the only things that had suffered.

Her breath came in tortured gasps through lips that used to be rosy smooth. Her eyes, which had been the clearest blue, were now bloodshot, wild, and watery. She could hardly see where she was stumbling. At least her hair was not in her eyes. It used to be that she would constantly shrug or push her long blond hair out of her way. But now her hair was almost gone. There was just a close-cropped yellow halo around her head. She didn't look like Barbara Steinbrunner, the nineteen-year-old "Snow Queen" of Berkeley. With all the welts across her body and the rude haircut, she looked positively punkish.

The outfit didn't improve the image. Her tight jeans, the Frye fashion boots, and the black turtleneck sweater which had shrunk, exposing some of her midriff, were gone. They had been ripped off long ago. Instead she wore a hospital gown. One of the embarrassing ones that tied in the back and was too short. She looked like a missing member of the Sex Pistols

Finally, the rain didn't help. It was a San Francisco summer shower—pelting her with cold, liquid gravel at 1:40 in the morning. Naturally Barbara didn't know what time it was. Her time had stopped. Ever since the two figures had emerged from the bushes near a campus utility shed in what seemed like eons ago.

She hadn't seen the men, but she did notice the thick, dark foliage around the small shack. It didn't register immediately, but she also saw an unusual shadow near the usually locked shed door. It made the doorway look wider. Only afterward did she realize that it only looked wider because the door was ajar.

They had come at her from two sides. The first grabbed both her arms just above the elbow and pulled. She fell back into him, but he kept pulling. Any initial cry she might have made was knocked out of her by the force with which her back hit his rock-hard torso. She was quickly collecting her breath to scream when the shadow of a second assailant loomed in front of her. She saw his arm move, then felt a horrible pressure across her stomach. What would have been her second cry came out of her mouth as a scraping wheeze.

She doubled over in pain, her mouth wide open and her arms straining forward. The grip above her elbows remained tight, so all her arms could do was wave weakly from side to side. Before the horror clamped over her head, she felt her fingers fluttering helplessly, like the dying wings of a butterfly caught in a spider's web.

Then the figure in front of her moved again. Next thing Barbara knew, a thick plastic sheet was covering her face. Before she could turn away, she heard a click, and the unctuous black goo attached itself to her head. It sucked onto her face like a leech, fastening her expression into place. She couldn't open her eyes, she couldn't close her mouth. Worst of all, she couldn't breathe.

As hard as she inhaled, no air could pass through the black plastic. She violently shook her head, but it was stuck to her face like a vise. She was then thrown forward so her arms were free. But before she could raise them to rip the thing from her face, another pair of arms wrapped around her torso, pinning her limbs to her sides.

She was lifted, carried a few steps, and dropped. She fell on her side, her arms out in front of her. The pain of her fall was inconsequential—all sensation had fled, replaced by the panic-ridden void of asphyxiation. She was suffocating, and she had to get the horrible clinging thing off her face.

Her hands moved unerringly toward her head. They were just about to touch the plastic when two other rough hands gripped her wrists. With a socket-wrenching jerk, her arms were pinned behind her back. She slammed over on her stomach. A knee nailed her there. She felt something soft and satiny slip over her hands. They felt like the softest of leather gloves. Then there was a tight, momentarily painful stricture at her wrists. Another sudden tug and her hands were together, palm to palm, and her arms making a tight "V" straight down her back.

It was a strange floating sensation. In just a few seconds her entire upper body was immobilized. It was as if she had been paralyzed from the waist up. She felt like she was floating. She was just about to enjoy the feeling when she realized it was because she was dying. She suddenly remembered reading about the death euphoria in psychology class with crystalline clarity. When air to the brain ran out, cells started to die, creating a feeling of dizzying rapture. Like when she was high.

Life had suddenly taken on an extra dimension, a sharpness it hadn't had before. She could feel every individual blond hair that was caught between her face and the tight plastic mask. She could feel the rocks and ground along her front. She could practically feel the men's fingerprints as they worked on her arms. She had a quick, last coherent thought. She was going to die with her mouth open.

As the thought ended, she was whirled over and sat up. She felt a centralized sensation between her legs and heard a moisture-ridden sucking sound. Then the rubber mask fell away. Air slapped her like the hand of an angry suitor. She closed her mouth to gasp, blinked, then opened her lips to get as much oxygen as she could. As she tried, another rubbery wad was rammed into her mouth. She felt something move down her tongue and spread out, pushing open her jaws until they would go no farther. Then she was spun over onto her front again. For the first time she heard one of her attackers speak.

"Get her fucking hair out of the way," he hissed.

Barbara's proud blond mane was bunched up in a man's hand, like spaghetti being twisted up in a fork, then pulled over to the side of her head. She felt a buckle being tightly secured on the back of her head, sinking two straps into her cheeks. She tried biting down. The thing in her mouth wouldn't give. She tried spitting it out, but the straps on her cheeks were attached to the buckle as well as to the gag. She screamed. It emerged from what space it could as a choked gurgle.

She was flipped over onto her back again. The night was finally given some delineation by her eyes. She could only just make out the silhouettes of her attackers toiling over her waist, but she could see herself. First she saw a hose attached to a squeeze-bulb coming out of her opened mouth. She saw her black, thin sweater stretched over the sturdy mounds of her breasts. She saw a thin, coiled leather rope stretched from between her legs to her belly button and tied around her waist.

She tried moving her arms. It pulled the rope along her pelvis even tighter. It started a heat inside her already tight jeans. As soon as she felt it she moaned, and the indignity, the humiliation, and the fear hit her like a battering ram. She had been attacked. She was in the darkened, deserted shed She was helpless.

She fought back as best she could. Her legs were not yet tied so she kicked with all her might. Bound as she was she couldn't get enough leverage to collect any power. The attackers had placed her in the middle of the floor, so she couldn't make noise by hitting the walls. The men moved back so she couldn't do any damage there.

Instead she writhed, kicked, and moaned. She made pitifully little sound in the small enclosed area. Anyone outside wouldn't have heard a thing.

"I'll get the van," she heard one of the men mutter. "You like this sort of thing more than I do."

"Yeah," said the other.

The first man moved over to the door, opened it slightly, and slipped out. Barbara twisted around to see him leave. The moonlight that came in during those few seconds was enough to expose the shed's interior. There was nothing inside she could use to get free. Just an empty cardboard box or two beneath the shack's one small window.

Barbara squirmed toward them. If she could just lean up against them or the wall, maybe she could gather her wits. She struggled up to her knees. She had put one booted foot flat on the floor when the other attacker moved over, put a hand on her shoulder and pushed her onto the floor again

"Uh, uh," he said with quiet relish, "none of that."

She twisted onto her side, raised her head, and looked at him. The blue moonlight coming in the window revealed his face. If not for the high cheekbones, it would have been a totally gentle, boyish face. The eyes were brown, the hair was thick and brown, and he was clean shaven. His skin looked almost soft. But his thick neck and strong cheekbones gave him away. There was muscle under that smooth, placid surface.

There was also perversion. Looking away for a moment, Barbara glanced at the window When she looked back, he was motioning at the glass with his head.

"Go ahead," he said, "I won't stop you."

She stared at him, her eyes widening with frightened confusion. What could they want? The wad filling her mouth and the mucous filling her throat made it hard to breathe. And the minimized air made it hard to think. She wasn't rich. She made just enough with her free-lance word-processing jobs to pay for tuition, rent, and food. Her parents weren't wealthy. Besides, they had all but disowned her after she went away to college. She hadn't written or talked to them in about a year and a half.

She couldn't understand it, and her confusion wasn't helped when the second man motioned at the window again.

"Go ahead," he said more as an instruction than a suggestion.

Her head was beginning to hurt. Moaning, she rolled over onto her stomach, brought both knees up under her and sat up. She was about to stand when the man behind her moved up, pulled off his belt, wrapped it around her thighs, just above her knees, buckled it tight and pushed her on her face a second time.

She cried out, only to hear a sodden sob as she painfully hit the ground. Her arms were useless to her—it was her breasts that took the brunt of the fall. She rolled over to see that his belt was a perforated kind that was popular in the sixties, one that could be buckled anywhere along its length. She looked up to see his smiling face.

"Now," he said soothingly, "go ahead."

She tried to plead with her eyes. They filled with tears and her breath came in sobbing bursts. His expression didn't change. Slowly, she rolled onto her stomach and crawled toward the window. He walked around her and watched her progress from the side. Twice she caught the squeeze-bulb hanging out of her mouth between the floor and her chest. And twice the pressure made the wad in her mouth spread even more. It was a hand pump, she realized. She had seen it in a doctor's hands when she was taking the blood pressure part of her yearly physical

Through the red-flecked haze in her head, she thought about all the captive heroines she had seen on television. For them, a scarf over the mouth or between the teeth were enough. At the very worst, their lips would be taped shut. But here the object was not to keep her mouth closed, but wide open. The pain and the effectiveness of the device was nearly overwhelming.

Finally her forehead touched the hewn wall of the shed. She was right below the window. She raised her aching head and looked up at it. It was a regular setup with four glass panes interrupted by two crossing pieces of wood. It could not be opened. She tried standing up. The belt binding her knees made it impossible. The bottom of her legs simply kicked out forward and back. Her ankle joint was no help since her fashionable, high-heeled boots didn't have much give.

"Good. Very good," whispered the man behind her. "You did that really, really well."

He walked behind her, pulled a box close to the window and sat above her. He then cupped a hand under her jaw and wrapped his other arm around her waist. He spread his fingers so his thumb went under her turtleneck and his pinky slipped under the waist of her jeans. He lifted her up onto his lap.

She sat on something hard and jutting. She tried to pull herself upward, but his hand tightened around her jaw, spreading to her neck. He slowly, strongly, eased her back down to his lap.

"There now," he said. "There, there now."

Barbara's terror was mingled with anger. He was talking to her like a baby or a pet dog. Always the most soothing, yet authoritative of tones. And the most caressing of hands. She could feel the strength of his fingers on her, but she could also feel the smoothness of his flesh. It stroked her face and warmly rubbed her stomach. She sat on his lap, her heels a few inches off the floor and her hair a few inches from the top of his head. She felt small and powerless in his clutches.

He enhanced that feeling by directing her gaze out the dirty glass pane. His fingers gripped her chin and twisted her chin in that direction. She could see the exit of the Science Building from the window as well as the entrance to the Student Union where she had been heading when she was attacked. And from where she was sitting she could see one or two other students going about their late-night campus business.

She started as she saw them. And just as she jerked forward, the attacker calmly placed one of his legs in front of the two of hers. She couldn't kick the wall, his leg was in the way. She couldn't butt the glass with her head, his hand was holding her back. She couldn't scream, the inflatable gag filled her mouth. She couldn't fight, the leather wrapping her hands which was bound to her waist by a leather thong kept them nestled against her rear end.

In desperate frustration, she struggled anyway. She writhed and shook in his grip. She bucked on his lap, throwing her head forward and back, trying to scream all the while. She contorted her hands, trying to pull free of the bindings. Her shoulders and torso vibrated with the

16

effort to escape. She felt sweat all over her face, saliva drooling out the corners of her mouth, and an aching heat between her legs.

"Oh, that's nice," she heard him whisper. "Oh, that's nice."

It was only then that she realized what she had been doing. She realized where her hands were and what effect they had on him when she wiggled them to get free. She realized that every time she moved her arms she tightened the rope between her legs.

Her mind started to give way to hysteria. She tried to stop, but she couldn't. She kept writhing in his grip. He only held her tighter on top of him. He started cooing continually. All she heard was his mutter as she looked out the window and shook uncontrollably.

When the young man stepped out of the Science Building directly across the street, she suddenly became stock-still. She stared directly at him as he looked away from her down the street. She felt her attacker's head nestled among her long hair at the back of her neck. He didn't know about the student. He just kept muttering soothing words and pulled her tighter on his lap.

Barbara strained forward, trying to reach the window as she gathered her breath for one explosion of sound. She was sure she could do it. She was sure she could get the other student's attention with one sudden noise loud enough to get through the glass partition. Then, if he looked close enough, he would see her in the darkness and go get help.

At that moment the student's head turned to look down the street in the other direction. For a split second Barbara had seen his eyes look directly at her from across the street. But he hadn't seen her. He had looked right through her. And after that, he began to cross the street in her direction.

Barbara leaned ever forward as her lips curled up and away from the saliva-slick padding. She pulled back her head to drive herself forward and call out.

She was just beginning to jerk herself forward when the arm tightened around her waist and the hand cupping her chin slapped across the bottom of her face. Her muffled shriek bubbled beneath his fingers, and her forehead trembled a hair's breath in front of the glass

"Don't worry," came the quiet voice of her captor deep in her ear. "He can't see us. He won't hear you. Now, now, don't worry."

And with that, he began rocking her on his lap and the hand around her waist slipped over her rope-belt and under her dark sweater to settle on one warm breast. He fondled her and rocked her and cooed to her while she watched the other student walk away oblivious. He coddled her until she could hardly breathe and her sight was colored by swashes of darkness. When she saw his partner's van turn the campus corner, she lost consciousness.

Barbara really didn't know what happened after that. She really didn't know what was happening now. All she could remember was the pain, the darkness, and the choking. She also recalled fighting and the sensation of falling, but after that, nothing. Nothing but a seemingly endless road that ravaged her bare feet and wound farther and farther into the twilight zone.

There was darkness all around her. She weaved from side to side, trying to follow the double yellow line in the center of the cement. Every time she got close to the forest bracketing the road, she pulled herself back. She wouldn't go into the woods. She was afraid of what might be waiting for her behind the trees.

So instead she ran along a dim yellow band in the rain. And while she ran, she tried to remember why she was doing it. But, strangely, all she could remember was smiling faces. She saw one especially gentle-looking man smiling warmly at her. She couldn't understand why that caring smile filled her with such dread.

Slowly, subtly, the gentleman's face was infused with light. Two white dots shone out of his eyes and grew until they looked like suns and blotted out the man's entire visage. Then the entire road was filled with the same light. Just in time, Barbara recognized them as car headlights, threw her arms across her head, and fell to the side.

Two thick steel radials marked the road just inches from her. The car swerved, smashed a headlight on a roadside tree, spun around, slammed its rear into another tree, and screeched to a halt five hundred feet down the road, pointing in the opposite direction.

"Holy shit!" said Danny Barnes as he pulled himself from under the glove compartment. "Did you see that?"

"Christ Almighty," Tom Stillman breathed, his white-knuckled hands still gripping the padded steering wheel of his Firebird.

"Come on," said Danny as he kicked open his door, vaulted out, and ran down the road.

"Christ Almighty," Tom said again, trying not to hyperventilate.

Danny ran to the huddled form of the blond in the hospital gown. The thin cloth was stuck to her skin by the rain, and the hem had hiked up over her hip. He grabbed her shoulders to roll her over. She responded by fighting and howling like a wildcat. They struggled in the rain, he leaning down, not loosening his grip on her shoulders, she on her bended knees, punching and scratching the best she could.

"Tom!" Danny yelled. "Tom! Come on and help me, will ya?"

The young man behind the wheel snapped out of his spell when he heard his friend's voice. He scrambled out of the car, glanced at the damage, then ran over to the fight.

"What the hell is this?" he exploded. "Who is this broad?"

"How the hell should I know?" Barnes spat. "She's drugged or something, I don't know. Crazy, out of her head. Give me a hand, will you?"

"Come on," said Stillman, waving an arm at the straining girl, "she's wearing a hospital thing. She must be an escaped looney or something."

"Jesus," Danny cried, pulling away from the crazed girl, "she bit me!"

"Leave her there, leave her there," said Stillman. "She's an escaped nut!"

19

Barnes looked down at the girl, now crying on the ground, as Stillman began to move hesitantly back toward his car.

"Come on," Tom repeated. "My dad is going to kill me when he sees the damage."

"We can't just leave her here," Danny contended. "Look at her."

Stillman watched as Barbara began to pull herself toward the side of the road, cowering in terror.

"She's not going to hurt anybody," Danny said.

"All right, all right," said the driver, coming back. "Let's get her out of here and over to a police station, OK?"

"OK," said the other boy, already moving toward the huddled feminine figure. Danny gingerly touched the girl's shoulders. Tom moved around her legs, carefully avoiding any proximity to her raw, swollen feet. He didn't want to get caught if she suddenly kicked out. As Barnes tried to get her up, Stillman took a good hard look at her.

"Hey, she's quite a looker, isn't she?" he remarked.

Danny looked at her naked hips then up at his friend's face.

"Pull down the skirt, huh, and help me with her, will you?" he demanded.

"OK, already," Tom complained, tugging at the hem of Barbara's hospital outfit. She looked up when his fingers touched the cloth. As he covered her pelvic area with it, she relaxed. After that, the Barnes boy had no trouble bringing her to her feet.

"We won't hurt you," he told her, standing in the rain. "Come on, you'll freeze out here."

They brought her over to Tom's Pontiac and opened the back door.

"I'll get in with her and try to find out where she's from," Danny said.

"Good luck," Tom replied, quickly sliding into the front seat behind the wheel. "Now let's see if I can get this thing started again."

Everyone settled in as Tom revved the engine. It caught hold and roared into a sputtering life. Danny stared at Barbara's face intently as she lay back, licking her lips and gulping. She was a beautiful girl, he thought, looking from her pretty profile to the strange wound on the back of her neck. It looked like a slight indentation— a bruise of many dark, swirling colors.

He looked down her well-shaped profile. The rain had made the gown all but translucent. He saw the breasts and waist perfectly outlined. They would heave up and down as she breathed deeply. He found himself thinking that it would be a shame to take her back to a hospital.

Tom put the car into gear and turned around. "Where to?" he asked.

"She was running in this direction," Danny said, tearing his eyes away from Barbara's figure. "Go back the way she came," he finished, pointing forward.

"Right-O," replied Tom, releasing the brake and pressing down on the accelerator.

When Danny turned his attention back to the girl, she had stopped sucking in air like a drowning woman and was lying back peacefully with her eyes closed. The rain had washed her face clean, and the heat in the car was already bringing some color back into her cheeks.

"Who are you?" Danny asked the still figure.

Barbara opened her eyes and turned her head toward him. Danny saw that her eyes were a light, liquid blue. But there was no comprehension in them.

"Who are you?" he repeated. "Where are you from?"

She continued to look at him with an expression that mixed innocence with ignorance. She opened her mouth slightly, but no words came out. She seemed surprised by her own silence. She opened her mouth wider. Danny could see the muscles in her neck working. But still no sound came out.

"We could always bring her home as a pet," Tom suggested from the front seat, looking at his friend's progress in the rearview mirror. "Wouldn't the guys at the frat love that."

Danny was about to reprimand him for his callousness when the girl began to react to what the driver had said. She looked quickly from the back of Stillman's head to Barnes' face, her eyes widening. Her mouth moved, but still there were no words. She gritted her teeth and swal-

21

lowed. Nothing. She began to get upset. She grabbed the back of the driver's seat and shook it in frustration.

"What is it?" Danny asked her, gripping her shoulders again. "What's the matter?"

"Get her off the seat, get her off the seat!" Tom yelled, the car swerving because of his surprise.

Danny quickly gripped her wrists and pulled her back. "There, there," he soothed. "Take it easy."

But his words only seemed to make the agitation worse. She began to buck in his grip, squealing incoherently.

"Jesus," Tom compained, "keep her quiet, will you? I'm going to hit the CB and find out if anybody else knows about her."

So saying, Stillman reached for his radio rig and set the wavelength. Danny wrapped his arms around the girl and held her against him. Her cries had diminished to a pitiful growling sound.

"Breaker, breaker, one-nine, anybody know about a lost girl proceeding north on Route 15? Over."

Stillman's only reply was static. Barbara stared at the CB, then started to screech.

"Shut her up!" Tom yelled, one hand on the wheel, one hand on the mike. "I can't hear a thing!"

Danny held her struggling form with one arm and put the other one over her mouth. As her kept her down and pressed her cries into a turbulent hum, Tom repeated the message. Barbara watched from the back seat with wild eyes. Again, there was no reply.

"There's nobody on the road for miles in this mess," Stillman concluded, disgustedly slamming the mike back onto the rig. "Let's drive onto 101 and find a state police station."

They moved forward, Tom doing his best to drive his wounded car through the rain, and Danny doing his best to calm his jittery passenger down. As soon as Tom had put the CB away, Barbara had stopped yowling. Danny had let her go, and she had slipped down to lie on the seat, convulsively crying.

"Whoo," Danny breathed, leaning forward to rest his

arms on the rear of the front seat. "She's pretty, but out of her head."

"I told you so," said Tom. "What's that?"

Stillman pointed and Barnes looked in that direction. Coming up the road was a big dark vehicle, outlined by six separate headlights dotting its entire front.

"Jeez, it looks like a UFO from *Close Encounters,*" commented Danny, as he watched it weave up the winding back road toward them. "What about it?"

Tom looked out the passenger window. Then he looked back at the oncoming vehicle. He switched on his headlights' high beams, then switched them off again. "Hey, we're on the right side of the road and so are they."

"So what?"

"I don't mean the right side of the road," stressed Stillman, "I mean the *right* side of the road! They're on our fucking side!"

Danny pulled himself over the front seat. "What are you talking about?"

"They're on the wrong side of the road, goddamn shitheads."

Danny looked closer. Sure enough, the vehicle was tooling through the rain directly at them.

"Pull over," he suggested to Tom.

"Hell," Tom replied, "I'll go around 'em." With that, Stillman pulled the car over into the left lane. Immediately after, the van moved over to straddle the double yellow line.

"Pull over!" Danny shouted.

Tom swerved to the right side and hit the brakes.

"No!" screamed the girl.

Both men whirled to look at her. Barbara's face was screwed up in intense pain, as if the one word had been torture to get out. The car's deceleration had dumped her between the front and back seat where she huddled, her mouth still desperately working.

"They'll . . . kill . . ." she managed to choke out. "Kill."

Tom looked out the front windshield. The six-eyed machine was still barreling toward them. Danny put his hand on his friend's shoulder.

"They'll pass. Let them pass."

Tom looked at the girl's expression, then back at the approaching vehicle. "I don't care what you think," he said, "but I'm getting out of here!"

The Firebird's engine roared its might to the wet night skies again, bit into the dirt by the side of the back road, and burned rubber backward. Its butt swung back onto the road just as Stillman spun the wheel and hit the handbrake. The big Pontiac swung around to face the other way. The driver stomped on the accelerator and sped off ahead of the chasing van.

Danny looked out the rear window. "It's right on our tail! It didn't slow down at all!"

Stillman swore under his breath, and looked in the rearview mirror. "I told you that chick was trouble," he mumbled, returning his gaze to the road with determination.

"It's just a bunch of joyriders," Danny said unconvincingly.

"Like hell," Tom retorted, beginning to weave back and forth across the narrow roadway. "They're after her."

"That's crazy," the boy in the back seat said, looking at the girl, whose eyes were closed again. "It makes no sense."

"What makes sense," Stillman spat, "is that we picked up a drugged girl in the middle of nowhere and as soon as we gave any sign of it on the CB, this monster behind us shows up."

Danny turned. Three of the vehicle's six eyes glowed into his face. "It's right behind us!" he shouted, turning back. "It's keeping right up with us!"

"Shit," said Stillman. "It must have incredible horsepower. Probably gets minus four to the gallon. I need a hill. Where's a fucking hill?"

Barnes knew what his friend was trying to do. If he could get on an upward incline the Firebird could take off, but the heavier van would have to shift down into a lower gear. But as far as he knew, they were on the wrong side of the hill. "It's all downhill from here," he said, then swung around to look at their pursuer just as the rear windshield exploded.

To Danny, it seemed to crack everywhere at once, sending the sound of lightning ripping through the car. Right afterward came the thunder—an ear-punching boom coming from the pursuing van. Then the glass flew in. Dozens of bright, sharp, whirling pieces spun into Barnes' face. All he saw was yellow and white stars, and all he felt was pain. He smashed back into the rear of the passenger seat, breaking its lock-back device and driving himself over into the front of the car. The rest of the glass fell onto the seats, harmlessly showering Barbara's bowed head.

Tom had instinctively ducked when he heard the sound and only turned in time to see Danny hurl himself down, his hands clutching his face. The wounded boy rolled toward the driver's seat, streams of blood beginning to drool between his fingers. Stillman wrenched his attention back to the road, slammed down the accelerator, and tore the Firebird into overdrive.

The sportscar responded by leaping away from the van like Road Runner speeding away from Coyote. Tom clamped his hands onto the thick wheel in the ten and three o'clock positions and drove like a man possessed. He ignored the rearview mirror, glancing only occasionally at his friend twisting in the back on the passenger seat.

"Danny!" he yelled. "Danny! Can you see? Are you all right?" He heard Barnes gasping for breath. "Come on, man," he continued, "can you see?"

"Fuck," said Danny. "Oh God, it hurts."

"Come on!" the driver shouted. "They've got guns, Danny. We've got to get out of here. I need your help!"

Danny just kept moaning.

"Come on!" Stillman repeated. "Stop it! I need your help!" He leaned over and grabbed one of Barnes' wrists. He pulled, and Danny's hands dropped from his face.

One eye was destroyed. It drooled from the socket intermingled with the blood. The rest of the face was lacerated. One side of his nose was pulpy. His bottom lip was split. Skin hung off his chin and cheeks like crimson streamers. The horrible face was framed in the yellow headlights of the chasing van.

Stillman had a hard time holding down his dinner. He had a harder time controlling the car. It careened completely across the road to the left and scraped along a stone wall. It ran over three mailboxes before Tom was able to get it back on the road again.

By then the major damage had been done. His sudden loss of control had reduced his speed so the van was able to creep alongside. He bounced off the stone wall only to bounce back off the side of the van. He drove forward at sixty miles an hour, two wheels on the asphalt and two wheels on the dirt and grass.

Tom swung the wheel and slammed the van broadside again. The big dark vehicle didn't budge. He swung it once more and held the Firebird there. The two machines ground against each other as they rocketed down the last section of the hillside road.

They were coming into a slightly more populated region, Stillman realized. If he could just hold on for a few more miles, he would be in civilization again. Then he could get help.

Danny had slid down to crouch on the floor of the back seat. Tom couldn't see the girl, but she hadn't made a sound since the rear window blew in. And Tom couldn't take the time to check up on her. He was having enough trouble just staying on the road. He turned the steering wheel another time, trying to edge the van aside. But even with all the Pontiac's power, the larger vehicle drove firm. Stillman couldn't push it over and he couldn't get around it.

A garbage can suddenly loomed up in his headlights. It rested near the road, right in front of the car. Tom couldn't avoid it, so he drove right into it. The container flew out in front of both racing machines, scattering junk all over the road and the windshields. The shit was so thick that Tom had to flick on the windshield wipers to clear the last of the stuff away.

Through the spoiled milk and other rancid liquid, he saw a parked car. A parked car right in front of him. Surprised and shocked, Stillman acted instinctively. He slammed on the brakes, pulling his car behind the van. The Firebird swerved out to the right, pointing the Pontiac right at the woods to the left of the roadway. Tom saw a space between two trees. He drove for them.

The car hit the slight roadside incline, vaulting across the remainder of the space in midair. It smashed down between the two target trees and tore off into the forest.

The trip got worse from there. Stillman took his foot off the accelerator completely since the wood was growing on an incline. An incline that sent the car bouncing down its face at forty miles an hour. The car leaped across the rocky ground, dribbling Tom's head against the car's ceiling. The wheel bucked in his hands as he furiously tried to keep the car from colliding with any obstruction.

The Pontiac blasted through the woods, shattering its headlights, ripping off branches and pulverizing rocks underneath.

Tom tore the wheel to the left, then to the right, narrowly missing tree trunks both times. He found himself careening right toward a wall of bushes. The car rammed through, its tires spinning on empty air. It leaped over a ditch and smashed down into a bumpy field.

All four shock absorbers were shot simultaneously. The springs were driven through the bottom of the casing, and the casings were driven through the body of the car. One tire exploded out, while another tore half off the axle. The hood tore open with such force that it cracked the windshield.

The rain coming through the broken window woke him up. Tom Stillman felt warmth on his forehead. When he opened his eyes, he saw a curtain of crimson. He didn't panic. He was too dazed. He raised his head. Through the red fog he saw the cracked glass and the upside-down Firebird design of his car hood looming up beyond. He wiped at his eyes. The back of his hand came away bloody but his vision cleared.

He looked out the side window. He saw the woods and the jagged tear in the foliage where his car had come out. He tried to open his door. It wouldn't budge. He looked back at the locking button. It was up. He tried to push the door open again. It still wouldn't give. The effort

27

made him woozy. He remained still for a moment with his head down. He heard a moan.

He turned around and saw Danny lying across the back seat, semi-conscious. His hands were away from his ruined face and the blood was bubbling over his opened mouth. Their crash must have ruptured something, Stillman realized. He looked above his dying friend through the broken rear window. In the distance there were some lights. He could see them plainly. There were some multicolored lights illuminating a rustic-looking building.

His view was slowly interrupted by a cream color. Tom squinted into focus the face of the girl. She had risen up from her position on the floor. Incredibly she seemed unharmed by the chase. But she retained the blank, pained expression the boys had found her with.

It made sense, Stillman reasoned painfully. The girl hadn't been badly injured by the crash because she was so vacuous, so wasted. She probably went limp during the worst of it, he figured, so she avoided the worst of it. It was too bad Tom couldn't claim the same. There was pain in his every movement. He tried to get up, but the wooziness hit him again. Instead he leaned back in his seat and let his head loll sideways. He found himself staring into six tiny eyes.

He blinked. The six eyes were getting bigger and brighter. The fuzz left his head completely. They hadn't escaped, he realized. The van was still coming for them. He turned his head quickly. The action almost cost him his consciousness again. But he held on long enough to lock eyes with the girl.

"Run," he said. "Run to the building and get help." He looked from her to the building out the rear window and back again. "Go get help," he pleaded.

Barbara slowly turned around. The building came into sudden sharp focus. She didn't know why but she abruptly wanted to get to the structure more than anything else in the world. Almost instantaneously she forgot about the two boys and pulled herself inexorably toward the light in the distance.

The girl scrambled out the back windshield, rolled to the ground, found her footing, and began to stumble off across the field. Tom watched her go, then rolled his head back to look out the side window. The van hadn't sped up after the girl had climbed out of the car. With any luck the Pontiac blocked the van's view of the escaping girl. Tom Stillman smiled. In his dazed, wounded state the girl's safety had taken on paramount importance. Ever since the rear window had been shot in, the young driver had written himself off. Thare was no way he could get away from a van full of killers.

So he replaced his own importance with the girl's safety. Almost unconsciously he had decided to save her at any cost. And this was it. Danny was bleeding to death on the back seat, and he himself had a concussion or something like it. But the van was still just crawling its way toward them, seemingly oblivious of the girl's progress toward the building at the edge of the field.

Tom leaned back, closed his eyes, and smiled. He waited, expecting to hear the van's engine coming closer. Instead he heard a crackling noise coming from inside the car. He looked around quickly, fearing a fire had broken out. The noise was coming from beneath the dashboard, but there was no sign of flame. The only new color was the red of two lit-up numbers on the CB. Stillman saw that the mike had been jarred loose and the power turned on by the crash landing.

"The quarry has been cornered," a calm, clear voice came from the radio speaker. "The product is on the way."

Stillman started at the sound. The message could have meant many things, but a chill of dread crept through his mind. It wasn't over yet, he realized. These people weren't after him, they were after the girl. And if they were after the girl, they must've been aware of her leaving the Firebird. To complete the picture, they wouldn't be approaching so slowly if they were worried about the safety of the building in the least.

Ignoring his addled pain, Stillman clawed at his seat-belt strap, using it as leverage. "Danny!" he shouted, "Danny! If you can hear me, get out! Try to get away!" Tom pulled up and started to crawl out of his open side window.

The cool night air and the rain swirled around his messed-up head. They washed the dried blood from his face and gave him new strength. He was halfway out when he saw the girl halfway across the field.

"No!" he shouted. "Don't!"

His voice boomed out and seemed to roll across the field in an echo. As the soundwave reached the girl, she hesitated. After another second, she turned.

"Not that way!" Tom continued to shout, holding onto the seat-belt strap with one hand and waving from side to side with the other. "Run into the woods! That way!"

As he shouted he saw the silhouette of a figure move toward the rear of the car from the side. The assailant moved in silently, looking like solid, dark mist. Something the shadow brought up shone slightly in the moonlight.

Danny Barnes had become accustomed to the excruciating pain. He had heard his friend's voice shouting. He had not made out the words, but he had gathered the strength and the momentum to sit up. He rose in the back seat as the shadow shoved a long, blue-metal rod through the open back window. The end of the rod completely covered Danny's ear. The shadow's hand moved and Danny's head disintegrated.

It was like science fiction. Tom hadn't heard a thing before he saw his friend's head puff up, split open, and spread out in every direction. It was as if someone had taken the lid off a food processor while it was mixing cranberries. The red liquid and dark solid matter splattered against the dashboard, the windshield, and Tom's pants. He saw a little spit out of the windshield's long crack.

All the strength went out of him, and he let go of the seat-belt strap. But he didn't fall. His arms hung down and his legs kicked out over the gore-splattered seat, but he stayed balanced on the side windowsill. The pain and pressure across his neck told him why. A thin wire wrapped under his chin was holding him up. And the two hands holding the wire kept pulling it tighter and tighter. Tom wanted to shout at the girl to keep going, but an overwhelming feeling of drowning interrupted his words. He died marveling at the sensation.

Barbara watched both boys die from across the field. She couldn't comprehend everything that was happening, but she could understand the horror. She knew they were being murdered horribly. She knew the killers would come after her next. The only thing she didn't know was who she was and why this was happening to her. Patches of memory would appear before her mind's eye, but she couldn't put them together. And worst of all, she knew she had the solution somewhere in her mind but something was keeping her from it. The same something that was keeping her from forming words.

She spun around and continued across the field toward the building. Once inside she could scream. She would get attention and be taken away. The killers couldn't get to her then. She decided to keep going and keep fighting the thing that was clouding her mind.

As she ran and the rain poured down harder, Barbara began to remember. First, she could picture her own face. After that, the haze at the corners of her vision dissipated. The pain in her legs changed from distant throbs to sharp stabs. She didn't know where she was, but she knew it was a field. She realized she had been drugged and that was stopping her from talking. But she also knew it was wearing off.

She pushed herself harder toward the building. She saw a door along a side wall. Hardly able to control her cramping muscles, she slammed up against it, feeling a thumping throbbing from inside. She clutched the door latch in both hands and twisted. The door swung open almost effortlessly.

Barbara fell from one nightmare into another. The rain and terror were replaced by undulating light and a huge volume of sound. Ignoring the sensual chaos, she threw herself inside and slammed the door. The noise of the closing door was distant. The noise of a screeching, throbbing beat had superseded it. Barbara focused on the interior of the building and saw a large room filled with people. They were everywhere, and they were all moving. They performed in a multicolored semi-darkness, moving constantly in flashes of dark light.

Dazed, confused, nearly exhausted, Barbara moved

toward them. She hobbled through the shimmying crowd, but they couldn't see her terror. Her shoeless feet weren't unusual since many other girls had thrown off their shoes to dance better. The drops of blood that fell from her battered body were lost on the pulsating red, blue, and green lights of the dance floor. The rest of the light show neatly masked her bruised skin, since it colored everyone's flesh with blankets of yellow, purple, black, and white. And the loud, driving music drowned out her pitiful, pleading mews.

Barbara fell back against the disco wall, her mind fogging and tears welling up in her eyes. She couldn't get anyone's attention. They were all in their own worlds. They wouldn't notice another weak, seemingly stoned-out punk rocker. Barbara felt her legs giving way when a hand reached out and rested on her arm.

A soft voice whispered something in her ear. She turned toward the sound, relief flooding her brain. The first thing she saw were gentle brown eyes set in a calm face with high cheekbones and dark hair. She turned to run but another person stood beside her. It was an affable, stocky, bald man in a two-piece suit. He smiled down on her. She tried to move forward, but their hands were all over her. The bald man had her in a bear hug. The gentleman had his arms around her shoulders.

They were slowly but definitely forcing her to the back of the room. Both kept up a steady flow of soothing conversation as they moved, allaying any suspicions the apathetic but active dancers might have. The pain in Barbara's head built up increasingly the closer they got to the rear of the room, until it almost became too much for her to bear. She opened her mouth to scream.

The gentleman grabbed what was left of her hair and pulled back. He rammed his own open mouth on hers and pushed his tongue down her throat. The bald man let go of the couple and opened a door. Wrapping his arms around her and maintaining the choking French kiss, the gentleman pushed the girl through the opened door. The bald man quietly closed it behind them.

Inside, Barbara was suddenly free. The arms let her go and the wet slimy mouth disappeared. She looked around

32

wildly. Everywhere around her were the dancing people. She could see them through wall-high panes of glass that made up the room. She ran up to the transparent wall, slamming her legs against a thigh-high set of electronic equipment. She leaned over the machines, banged her fists on the wall, and screamed.

The volume of the scream was extremely loud, the pitch was extremely high, and Barbara nearly fainted with happiness that she had finally gotten it out. She blinked the tears out of her eyes and waited for a reaction. Nothing happened. She watched in horror as the dancers continued as if nothing had happened. It made her mind snap back.

She remembered everything—who she was, what had happened to her, and what it meant that the dancers couldn't hear her. In shocked resignation she looked behind her.

She was in a soundproof disc jockey's booth. A disc jockey's booth filled with the latest electronic gadgetry and the latest in one-way glass. She could see out, but no one could see in. No one could see her except the gentleman, another pair of men, and the seated woman at the disc jockey's turntable.

"Please," Barbara said hoarsely, "please don't bring me back to the cave."

The gentleman smiled. The two other men looked to the seated woman. That woman ignored Barbara while she gave her instructions.

"She's been touched," the woman said, as if Barbara was a bird who had fallen out of the nest. "A more permanent disappearance will have to be arranged." She looked down intently, then "tsked" with her tongue on the back of her upper teeth. "A tape is running. The music will not have to be changed for another forty-five minutes," she said to the room more than to any particular person. "I think we can find a way to turn this inconvenience into a benefit." She looked from one man to the other. "Go ahead," she finished lightly.

Barbara ran for the door. The gentleman caught her right arm, spinning her to face the other pair of men. They charged her, pinning her to the wall. The man on

33

the left pulled out and flicked open a switchblade. With a quick swipe, he cut her hospital gown all the way down the front. They pulled her to a console as the cloth fell away from her like an opening night curtain. The console was shaped so that her back arched over the top, exposing her torso completely. Barbara made little noises of struggle, but she was still too shocked to get a grip on herself.

The grip was supplied by the gentleman, who secured both arms behind her. She sealed her lips together and closed her eyes as the other men began taking off their pants. She started gasping as the first man approached her. He kicked her legs apart like a rude cop about to frisk a suspect. He leaned over her and started to work.

Barbara was too weak to fight back anymore. She remembered that this wasn't the first time this had happened since her abduction, but she couldn't look. She turned her head to watch the dancing throng continue mindlessly. Soon the pain became too much. In spite of herself she started to cry.

The men ignored her. They were too involved by this time to care. The woman simply got up, opened a drawer on the console, pulled out a sponge and a thick handkerchief, wrapped the sponge in the cloth, and drove it deep between Barbara's lips.

"Now, now," said the gentleman. "I'm sure we can find something more useful to do than that." The other men laughed as they turned the girl over on her stomach. The gentleman took ahold of her hair again and raised her head as one of the other men moved in. He removed the cloth, then rammed a wide metal ring under her teeth and buckled a strap attached to the ring behind her head. It kept her mouth wide open without filling it. The filling would come soon enough.

Barbara had one last coherent thought. She was going to die with her mouth open.

And then the three men raped and murdered her to the disco beat.

Chapter Two

San Francisco Homicide Inspector Harry Callahan rammed the barrel of his .44 Magnum revolver through the teeth of José Quintero Ramirez, lodging most of the metal firmly inside his cheek. Then the tall police officer swung his gun around, hurling the man down a flight of nine wide marble steps. All the years of brushing and dental floss did Ramirez no good at all as his enamel and gold followed him down the stairwell. Harry didn't even look back as he moved past the main entrance to the Steinhart Aquarium.

"Jesus, Harry," said Fatso Devlin, puffing alongside his partner. "All he said was 'Can I help you?' "

Harry grinned grimly, keeping up his quick pace, then spit into a corner of the lobby. Actually spit.

"Harry," huffed Devlin, "you're losing your objectivity." Then they were inside. As Fatso took in the incredible array of aquatic creatures in the vats and wall displays that littered the first floor and tried to get accustomed to the soft blue light, he had to admit to himself that this was a case to lose your objectivity on. Finding an eleven-year-old girl curled up dead in a garbage can was bad enough, but then to discover that she was a victim of a child pornography ring was enough to get the most seasoned cop mad.

And make no mistake. Harry was mad. When Harry was mad he did things like breaking people's faces. But only when those faces belonged to known members of the pornography gang. It had taken six weeks of intensive investigation to make sure Ramirez was part of the gang, so if a smart lawyer got him off the rap, at least Harry had the satisfaction of putting a big hole in his smile. It would be a while before José enticed any more children with those pearly whites of his.

But Ramirez was just the scum on the bottom of the rock. There were a few more members to run down. Namely Ted Cunningham, Earle Snelson, and Bobby Gagne. All three worked at this complex: the California Academy of Sciences—a perfect place to bring a child without drawing any attention. It was made up of three attractions, the Science Museum, the Morrison Planetarium, and the Aquarium, which Harry was presently scanning.

Cunningham worked there as a scuba diving instructor and fish feeder who would dive into the main pool at set times during the day. Gagne had the job of cleaning up after him, so they both usually holed up together in a locker room on the third floor. Harry hit the stairs while Fatso moved toward the elevators. The entire place was surrounded so neither worried very much about escape; all they hoped was that somebody tried to resist arrest.

Harry lucked out the very first time. He kicked open the locker room door, even though it wasn't locked, and pointed his big revolver straight down a row of lockers. He had timed his attack perfectly. Both men were there, Cunningham half into his scuba outfit.

"Freeze," Harry shouted, looking as crazy as he could.

Cunningham was the slick one. He followed orders. Gagne was the jerk. He panicked and ran.

"Jesus Christ, you fool!" Cunningham screamed after him. "Hold it, hold it!"

Harry punctuated Cunningham's outburst with a burst

of his own. He fired the Magnum right through the open locker door. Even though the distance was at least twenty feet, the high-powered hunk of lead went through the thin metal without throwing the door back. It made a hole almost an inch wide and ripped off the shirt cloth from Gagne's elbow as he ran.

Harry looked to his left. The locker room was fairly big, with three rows of lockers ending with a wall of scuba and feeding equipment. From where Harry was standing he could not see another exit, but that didn't mean there wasn't one. Harry pointed his gun at Cunningham.

"Don't go anywhere," he warned.

"Not me," said the diver, both hands up.

Harry moved quickly to the left. A moving target was better than a too cautious one. Just as he hopped from the cover of the first locker row to the second, there was a whipping, springing sound and a spear shot over his right shoulder and ripped sparks off the concrete wall behind him. Callahan immediately leaned to the right and fired. The bullet tore the spear gun in half but Gagne was gone again.

"Don't be an idiot, Bobby," Harry heard Cunningham call out. "He's got us dead to rights. Come on out so the good cop can take us in."

Harry didn't like the sound of that. Especially since Cunningham's voice was coming from a different place than Harry had left him. Rather than hazarding another hop between rows, Harry moved silently back to the first locker row. He looked around the corner of them to see Cunningham turning the corner at the other end. On the bench where he had been sitting was a box of shells.

So good old Ted came to work prepared with a weapon in his locker. Harry sadly shook his head and quietly slipped in two new shells to replace the spent ones. Then he moved down to where Cunningham had been sitting. He made a mental calculation of how far the bench was from the locker, how tall the lockers were, and what kind of effort it would take to vault them. Then he looked at the ceiling.

There were fire faucets along a pipe just under the

cement ceiling. Harry reached into his tweed jacket pocket for a pack of matches. He stood on the bench while bending a match to rest against the flint strip in his hand. He put that in his left hand under the fire faucet and held onto his Magnum with his right. With a flick of his thumb and forefinger the match was lit. He loosened his grip so the match could burn down and set the whole pack aflame. As soon as they flared, the water came on.

The sudden indoor shower got the reaction Harry was hoping for. One of the men swore. Harry pinpointed the voice in the next aisle. He hopped off the bench, ran back, and shot two Magnum bullets through the lockers in the voice's general direction. He ran right after the bullets, leaped onto the bench again, and vaulted up to the locker tops. He landed flat on his stomach just in time to see Gagne blasting at the lockers with his own gun. He was shooting at where he thought Harry was. Harry shot him from where he actually lay.

Bobby was thrown back, the back of his knees catching on the second aisle's bench. His head swung down to slam against the closed locker doors with a sound that would make a bell ringer proud. He bounced off that, his legs unfurled from the bench, and he slammed to the cement floor, still and silent.

Harry hopped down, keeping a wary eye out for Cunningham. He was the crafty one of the group. He wasn't the boss, but he was the closest thing to it they would find here. He heard the door slam. Callahan ran back to the entrance, pushed it open as he passed, then flattened himself on the wall next to it. Two bullet holes popped open in the wood of the door from outside. Cunningham was on the run, armed and dangerous. Harry shouldered his way through the door after him.

He saw Cunningham slamming open the exit door to the roof. Harry walked slowly after him just as the elevator doors opened and Fatso stepped out.

"You sure work up a sweat, don't you?" he said, seeing Harry's dripping wet face and soiled suit.

"There's one back there who won't give you any trouble," Harry told him, motioning toward the locker room.

38

"Cunningham's on the loose with a sidearm and half a wet suit."

"Which half?" asked Devlin.

"The bottom half," replied Harry. "So you'll have no difficulty recognizing him."

Devlin nodded and pulled out his walkytalky to report to the forces outside. Harry moved on to the roof door.

Thinking better of opening it and walking out, he stepped over to the window to take a look first. As far as he could see was a flat, white-graveled roof flanked on two sides by different sections of the building. Beyond that was Golden Gate Park, the Music Concourse, and the De Young Museum. Cunningham was nowhere to be seen. Harry cursed under his breath. If a half-naked man wearing rubber pants and waving a gun could be lost, the rest of the SFPD could probably do it. Taking a deep breath, Harry pushed open the roof door and stepped out.

Nothing happened until he was midway to the roof edge. Then several little fountains of rock dust gouted up, stinging his legs with gravel shards. Harry ran, rolled, and came up against the side of the building. No more bullets were forthcoming. The attack had told him three things. First, the guns had to be automatics since there were no loud reports following the richochets. That meant they were silenced weapons, and only automatics could be silenced effectively.

Second, the shooting had to be from some distance away. Otherwise he would have been hit by at least one of the shots. Even taking into consideration the lack of accuracy a silenced automatic causes, the attackers would have to be almost out of range not to hit a target as big as him. And lastly, more than one shooter had him sighted. The bullets had come from two directions. That meant that Earle Snelson was somewhere nearby.

Harry edged along the side of the building until he reached the edge. Looking down, he saw the large cylindrical pool that housed the sharks. The management thought it was best not to keep them inside. Rather, they had built an outdoor pool that flanked the building so an observation window could be utilized. That way, the patrons inside could feel safe looking at the sharks outside.

Callahan felt anything but safe. It was a twenty-foot drop to the ground and only a few feet of pavement separated the building side and the sunken shark pool. As dangerous as the man-eating fish were, it was hardly more risky than remaining on the roof. Whatever the case, Harry figured, he wasn't getting anything accomplished. So deciding, he left the security of the wall and stepped out into the sunlight.

The bullets began again. First one from his left, then another almost in front of him. But to fire on him, the others had to show themselves as well. Harry saw Cunningham let off a shot from an outcropping on the left corner and the slug went behind his neck. Snelson was behind some boxes in an indentation to the right of the roof door, and his lead dug into the roof between Harry's feet.

Harry answered both shots with shots of his own. The first whined off the wall Cunningham was behind and the other dug into one of Snelson's protecting boxes, followed by an insidious clank. Harry was fucking stunned. Snelson had hidden behind some scuba supplies.

Cunningham leaned out and peppered the roof with shots. Harry felt the heat of one across his cheek as he ran to the edge of the roof, jumped as high as he could straight up in the air, spun around and squeezed off three shots from his .44 at Earle's protective boxes.

As Harry fell, a shattering explosion ripped across the roof. Harry landed on his feet, fell sideways and rolled as hunks of wood and shards of metal flew out and down. As Harry threw himself against the wall away from the shark's pool, Snelson's ragged corpse bounced off the edge of the roof and somersaulted into the sharks' pool. One of Harry's high-caliber slugs had ruptured a scuba tank, causing it to explode from pressure. This probably did the other tanks absolutely no good at all. It was a good thing the police department had scheduled this attack early in the morning before any of the paying public could enter.

That way no one was shocked by the explosion and no one but Harry witnessed Snelson's broken body being attacked by the sharks. What little fluid he had left had spread out in the clear blue water, sending the sharp-toothed animals into a blood frenzy. Each animal bit down and tore another hunk off the already rended criminal. Within seconds there wasn't enough Earle Snelson to fit in a wallet.

Two down, Harry mentally calculated, one to go. He ran over to the side of the building where Cunningham was last hiding. He was in time to see the man run back inside the aquarium. Harry figured he must have been knocked from his perch by the blast, then figured to lose his police tail by getting lost in the exhibits. Harry followed his trail until he was back in the lobby. Police escorts and hospital orderlies were taking care of Ramirez and Gagne.

"Seen a man in wet suit trousers?" Harry asked an officer.

"No one sir," the cop replied as Devlin approached from the lobby elevators.

"What the hell was all the racket about, Harry?" his partner inquired.

"Snelson," Harry replied. "All over the place."

"Oh shit, Harry, where is he?"

"In the pool."

"I passed the pool. I didn't see anybody."

"Digested," explained Harry.

"Oh shit."

Callahan walked back to the first floor exhibits as Fatso sat on the steps, his head in his hands. "Didn't you see any blood?" asked a uniformed man. "Sure," said Devlin, "the water was red but I thought it was some new sort of cleanser or something." He looked after Harry's exiting figure. "I should have known better."

"He's the one they call Dirty Harry, isn't he?" the cop asked.

Devlin nodded. "Now you know why," he told the uniformed man.

Dirty Harry Callahan went after the last child pornographer. If the cops hadn't seen Cunningham and he wasn't on the main floor, about the only logical place to go was down in the cellar where all the water-filtering equipment was running. It was about the only place to get really lost when the rest of the place was crawling with cops. Harry found the door and started to go down the steps.

The country is filled with aquariums, and they are all different shapes and designs. But when one gets to the basement, they really aren't that different. The exhibits need a fine filtering system, and the cellar is the logical place to put it. So almost all aquarium cellars are thin, low ceiling mazes of pipes, wooden walkways, shimmering pools of lightly vibrating water, and cement shells painted light blue.

The Steinhart structure was no different. Harry entered an aqua cavern of waving shadows. The liquid reflected everywhere, giving the impression that the whole basement was under water. Things seemed placid. Harry knew it wouldn't remain that way for long. He pulled an autoloader out of his pocket to keep it at the ready.

The San Francisco cop sidled lightly down the thin walkway, made all the more narrow by a row of water pools rising three feet off the floor and wild systems of drainage pipes lining the walls, ceiling, and floor. Harry listened intently for any signs of life besides the drip-drip-drip of liquid.

He transversed the whole first hall, discovering nothing. As he rounded the bend he found the floor completely covered by six pipes. A makeshift catwalk had been set up consisting of several boards placed side by side atop some cinder blocks. The area was lit by one, low-hanging, naked white light bulb, so the shadows of waves were more stark than before.

Harry cautiously stepped up on the wooden planking and started down the passage. Halfway he wondered whether or not he had guessed wrong. Even though the cellar looked complicated, there was really very little place to hide. And unless Cunningham was waiting in ambush around the next corner, he wasn't in the basement at all. But still, it made perfect sense—there was no other place for the bastard to go.

Callahan looked at the cement rectangles that held the draining water along the right wall. He looked at the pipes to the left. His hair was scraping the ceiling. He looked down just in time to see the figure under the boards move.

Two 9mm slugs tore through the planks and slapped off the low cement ceiling as Harry fell sideways into the nearest shallow pool. He couldn't afford to worry about his pride or his suit. If he had merely hopped aside, he'd still be in sight and the ricochets could do some damage. He had no sooner splashed down than he was pushing himself up and returning fire. The sound of his Magnum was deafening.

The .44 slugs punched out whole sections of the boards and whined off of the underlying pipes. Cunningham had slid down the hall on his back and tumbled out from the catwalk at the far end. He stood and fired another silenced shot at the crouched, soaking wet policeman. The bullet sent up a little fountain to Harry's right. Harry pulled up his gun and had the wet-suited figure stuck on the end of the barrel for a split second. He pulled the trigger. Nothing happened.

Cunningham ran while Harry cursed. The tall cop saw his auto-loader on the bottom of the pool as he threw himself out of the water and barreled down the hall. Around the next corner was an exit door. It had almost swung closed when Harry reached it. He hurled it open and attacked a short flight of stairs. The stairwell was one of those infuriatingly narrow, short ones that made you turn a corner and move up in the opposite direction every six steps.

Callahan took them two at a time, his soaked, heavy clothing keeping him from going any faster. By the time he rounded the fifth corner, he felt his breath getting heavy, but he also saw Cunningham just turn for the sixth time. As Harry pivoted around the corner and plunged ahead, he saw the door at the top of the stairs. He took the last set of steps while pulling out the second of his three auto-loaders and jamming the rounds in the gun's cylinder. His shoulder hit the door just as he swung the revolver shut.

The door opened up onto the lobby of the planetarium. And the planetarium was open for business. Already busloads of kids from area churches and playgrounds were filling up the large, long room. Moppets of all kinds were milling apart, herded by counselors of all types. Everybody under the age of thirty seemed to be there, except for a man in the bottom half of a diving outfit.

Harry stalked up and tapped on the first semi-adult shoulder he could find. A bearded, chubby, black-haired young man with glasses turned around.

"You see a guy with rubber pants around here?" Harry asked.

The bearded fellow had the look of any harried baby-sitter trying to tend more than a dozen monsters at once and was about to abruptly tell Harry off until he saw the gun.

"That way," the young man said, staring at the Magnum and pointing at a set of eight swinging doors. "Right that way . . . sir."

"Thanks," said Harry, already heading in that direction. He ignored the shouting lady at the ticket taker's counter who was saying something about how the show had already started. Harry opened the door a bit anyway and slipped inside.

He was just in time to veer dangerously near a glowing nebula. The audience, seated in a circle and staring up at the dome above them, gasped as Harry slid along the circular wall. Their faces glowed as they neared the bright, shimmering collection of stars. Harry took in each of the faces as best he could. As far as he could tell, Cunningham was not sitting down.

Then Harry spied a security guard a little farther down the wall. The thin, unarmed, uniformed man was staring up in as much rapture as the seated kids. Harry took up a position close to the fellow's ear.

"Is there another exit in here?" he asked, motioning his head at the doors he had just entered from.

"Naw," whispered the security guard. "We don't want anyone to sneak in."

"Uh-huh," said Harry. "Enjoy the show."

"I never get tired of this stuff," said the guard, even

after Harry had moved away from him. "Have a nice day."

Harry started checking out all the aisles. The place wasn't sold out so early in the morning so there was plenty of room to search.

"There are millions of nebulas throughout our galaxy," a sonorous voice boomed down from the projected heaven as Harry stalked his prey in the semi-circular rows. "Just as there are millions of stars and planets, there are billions of these beautiful masses of gases throughout the universe. And among the stars, there are thousands growing old and going nova every single second of every single day. . . ."

As the omnipresent voice spoke, the picture on the curved ceiling changed again to a pulsating red sun which seemed to burn down the very walls. The crowd gasped again, and the entire place looked like the inside of a photographer's developing studio. And just as the picture changed, a hunk of the seat that Harry had laid a hand on, spun off into his stomach.

The cop fell flat on his face. Now he knew Cunningham was in the planetarium and still had a loaded automatic with a silencer.

The picture above him changed again as the bodiless voice explained, "Dying suns come in two categories; the red giant and the white dwarf . . . ."

As the white dwarf was given shape, Harry risked sticking his head up and checking the chair's damage. The missing piece was knocked off from across the room and to the right, if Harry was any judge of bullet trajectory. But by now Cunningham would have changed his position. The bastard could spend the whole show shooting from the cover of an unknowing kid in the audience until he finally pegged Callahan. Harry decided not to risk it.

It was getting to the security guard's favorite part when he felt the tug at his pant leg. He looked down, expecting to see a lost little girl or boy. Instead, he saw a big, craggy-faced man in a damp tweed jacket lying on his back. Smiling pleasantly, the man motioned the guard to lean down.

Ted Cunningham looked over the top of a seat across the theater and saw only the back of a tourist's head. He scrutinized the entire area, looking for any sign of Harry Callahan. All he saw was the security guard slowly leaving the dome room through one of the eight doors on the opposite wall. Cunningham wondered whether it was possible his one shot had caught the homocide inspector after all. He remembered seeing the chair back break off and Harry go down. With the strength of his automatic, it was possible that the bullet went through the wood and into the cop's stomach. God knew the silenced weapon was heavy enough. Maybe the security guard had discovered Callahan's body and was going to report it without raising a general alarm.

The criminal took a second to look down at the long dark weapon in his hand. The Browning automatic looked like a miniature Howitzer in his hand. The fourteen 9mm rounds in its clip weren't incredibly accurate, especially with the silencer which added almost three inches to its snout, but what it lacked in aim, it made up for in power and intimidation. With it, he had made a few of his pre-teen "charges" wet their BVDs and cream in their Sergio Valentes.

Cunningham looked up again and smiled. If the bullet had hit Callahan anywhere on his torso, the cop would be down for the count. And with Harry out of the way, it would not make any difference how many cops were surrounding the place or how many would charge the planetarium to back him up. Good old Ted would be long gone. If anybody asked, all the regular help would say that there was only one way to enter or exit the theater. But Cunningham worked there. Only he and the planetarium director knew about the director's booth.

That was the core of the entire dome show. That was where the experts worked up and controlled the action on the computers. That was where the sound and lighting equipment was. And that was where an ample air-conditioning duct was. Cunningham knew he could slip in the theater door to the director's booth, make some excuse to the controller, and make good his getaway.

Even if Harry wasn't dead, he couldn't stop Cunningham now. He wouldn't know how. The air-conditioning pipes were big enough to let Cunningham slide and crawl to the outside. He would get out a second exit no one knew about.

As Cunningham hitched up his rubber slacks and crawled for the other side of the room, Harry Callahan stuck his head up a third exit. He had snaked out the theater on his back and sat down with the custodian just outside the theater. Fatso Devlin had showed up, and Harry, explaining the situation, had him place a small army outside the main doors.

"He's in there with a weapon and several dozen kids. I don't want the whole thing to turn into a shooting gallery."

"OK, Harry," Devlin had agreed. "We'll surround him."

"I don't want a hostage thing on my hands either," Harry had countered. "I just want the place secure so if I don't luck out at least you have him boxed in."

"What do you have in mind?"

"Me and Max here," Harry explained, nodding toward the smiling custodian, "have an observation post picked out for me. If I see Cunningham I'll bring him down. If not, good luck."

"Thanks," Devlin had said laconically.

"Least I could do," said Harry, motioning that Max should lead the way.

"Harry . . . ?" Fatso called after him.

Harry turned.

"Don't make too much of a mess. You know how I hate cleaning up after you."

So Max led the inspector to the long, flat room of electronic machinery under the dome theater. He had brought Harry beneath the pit where the $140,000 projector was hung. Max had silently pulled open the bottom of the pit so Harry could stick his torso up directly under the dumbell-shaped device. Harry was just tall enough that his eyes looked over the crest of the pit. The bottom section of the projector was just above his head, its

47

concentrated light masking him from the crowd. But while they couldn't see him, he could see them just fine.

"Soaring throughout our galaxy are packs of comets," intoned the show's continuing narration. "These interplanetary hoboes range in size from the smallest of specks to the most incredible of satellites. Many are even bigger than the Earth. . . ."

On that word, Harry saw Cunningham. The man was crawling from the end of one row, across a carpeted aisle and into the same row on the other side. Harry looked in front of the creeping crook to guess his destination. It was easy. Besides the entrance, there was only one other door. Harry pulled his Magnum out.

"These gigantic hunks of compressed ore speed throughout the heavens," continued the melodic voice from the theater's speakers, "always moving in the same long orbits. As we see them through our telescopes in the night sky, they are cold and grey. We call them comets. . . ."

Callahan propped the barrel of his .44 on the lip of the pit. He sighted it along the row of chairs Cunningham was worming behind. He moved it along the lip at the speed he guessed his target was moving at. The barrel passed several innocent sitting figures looking happily up at the increasingly dazzling show.

"But when any of these hurtling stones reach our atmosphere," the narration continued, "and start to flame and burn from the air around them, we call them meteors . . !"

And the planetarium theater lit up with the blaze of projected falling meteors. The audience cried with delight. Cunningham took it as a cue to make a break for the director's room door. He hopped up with his back to Harry and started climbing over the three sets of rows in front of his goal. Callahan quickly realigned his aim and checked to see that no innocent person was close to his field of fire.

The Magnum barrel was pointed right at the middle of Cunningham's back as the man scrambled over the final row of chairs.

"Many meteors have struck the Earth during recorded history," the disembodied voice above Harry stated. "Incredibly, the daily count often reaches close to one hundred million. Most of these burn up harmlessly . . . but some . . . some have, and some will, strike the Earth with the force of fifty atom bombs! What will happen then?"

The audience held its breath in anticipation. Even Cunningham hesitated, pivoted, and looked up. Harry heard a fiery, crackling whooshing sound above him and felt a slight heat on the back of his neck. The projector was getting hot. Above him, a five-mile-wide meteor was coursing toward a fragile-looking blue marble. When the marble became the Earth and the meteor an orange ball of molten fury, Callahan barked out his order.

"Cunningham! Hold it!"

The man pinpointed the voice immediately He stuck his Browning out in front of him. Harry tightened his right forefinger. Both guns fired the moment the meteor smacked into the planet.

Cunningham's bullet gouged a foot long tear in the carpet in front of the projector pit. No one noticed the cough of his silencer. Harry's weapon boomed over the crash of the meteor, sending stabs of flame out at the edge of the projector pit. Its lead caught Cunningham in the right shoulder, a shot Harry prided himself on. There were two things Dirty Harry really knew how to hit—the right shoulder and right between the eyes.

The bastard spun into the wall, a full two feet off the ground. His Browning flew out of his hands, slid along the curved wall for a few yards, then fell neatly into a garbage can at the end of an aisle.

The lights came on and the narrating voice hoped everyone had enjoyed the show. The excited audience left the theater happy; only a few stopped momentarily to wonder why there were so many cops outside the doors and why the big guy in the wet tweed jacket jumped on the back of the man lying on the back-row carpet.

Chapter Three

"Really great job, Callahan," Captain Avery said sarcastically. "Water damage on the third floor, the second floor roof looks like the surface of the moon and the Aquarium experts are afraid their sharks might get sick from eating one of the alleged perpetrators." The blond, muscular police officer put his fists on top of his big dark oak desk and hung his head. "Eaten. Holy Mother of God."

"I really think you're being a bit harsh on the Inspector, sir," Lieutenant Al Bressler suggested from his standing position next to Harry in front of Avery's desk. "He captured all four of the suspects in a potentially explosive situation . . . ."

"*Potentially* explosive?" Avery burst out. "Callahan *never* wastes the potential of any situation! If there's anything to destroy, the Inspector will do it!"

Bressler loked at Harry, who raised his eyebrows and sighed. "I'm sorry for the poor choice of words," the lieutenant began back to the captain.

The captain interrupted. "Do you have anything to say about this, Callahan?" he barked.

Harry shrugged casually. "If you don't like results, sir. . . ."

"Results?" Avery cried, pouncing on the word. "You wound all four of the suspects, close down two of the city's most prosperous attractions in the middle of the summer vacation period, and cause untold damage, and we're no farther along than when you started on this case!"

Harry looked honestly confused. "How can that be?" he asked. "We've captured four of the pornography ring's major members. One of them is bound to talk."

"How can they talk?" Avery countered. "One's dead, one is in serious condition, and the other two are in the hospital's intensive care unit one with a destroyed shoulder and the other with a mushed mouth. The only talking they'll do is to their lawyers about suing the city for using excessive force! We're no closer to The Professor now than we were at the beginning of the investigation. If anything, this hunting trip of yours will probably send him underground, and we'll never find him."

"The Professor is a sadist," Harry said with conviction. "He won't stay under long. He likes what he does. The loss of four gang members won't stop him."

"You're guessing, Callahan," Avery said. "You've got no guarantees. I want *tangible* results, Inspector."

"You've got three men in custody, sir," Bressler mentioned.

"Who do us almost no good!" Avery retorted brusquely. "You want to know what we have that's tangible? I have a bill here from the Academy of Sciences. You want to know how much the damages were . . . ?"

"No, Captain," Harry interrupted suddenly. "You call up the parents of that eleven-year-old girl we found in the garbage can with a vagina that looked like hamburger. You tell them the cost and ask them if they think their daughter was worth that much."

Harry didn't wait for a reply. He turned around, walked out of the captain's office, and left the door open.

Avery's heavily lined face settled slowly down. The lines that had been arched upward drifted into a sloping position. He looked down at the bill sadly and fought the urge to crumple it. Instead he let it drop to his desk and sat down heavily.

"Close the door, Lieutenant," he instructed Bressler, "and let's talk."

Harry went back to his office in Room 750 on the seventh floor of the Justice Building. The Homicide department was in its regular uproar. It was the summer murder season, and people were getting croaked with their normal regularity. One nice thing about San Francisco was that it really didn't have any seasons. The average mean temperature for January was fifty degrees. The average mean temperature for August was sixty degrees. So it wasn't like New York where murder became epidemic in the summer and settled into dull slaughter in the winter. San Fran was constant, averaging a regular rate of homicide all year round. The only drawback was that things never really let up. Room 750 always had something to keep its occupants entertained.

Like the little girl in the trash can. Normally, pornography rings were handled by the vice squad. The eleven-year-old girl who had become a week-old corpse made it the Homicide department's business. Callahan moved back to his office to continue working on the case. Avery or no Avery, Harry was going to put as much time as he could on this one. It irritated his sensibility.

He wearily passed by all the other inspectors' cubicles to enter the Inspector #71 cubicle. Seated behind his grey desk was Fatso Devlin. Seated on the edge of the blue trim was an extremely pretty brunette. Now, some brunettes were beautiful, like Leslie Ann Down; all sultry and rich. And some brunettes were just pretty, like the Mary Ann character on *Gilligan's Island*. But this woman was extremely pretty: with creamy skin, full, perfect lips, and, to top everything else off, dark green eyes.

She was wearing a plaid shirt with a dark blue suit. The very edge of the shirt's collar was fringed with a quarter inch of lace. Her smile was terrific, very fresh and honest and she was using it on Devlin when Harry walked in. When she turned and noticed him, then lightly hopped off the desk edge and walked toward him with her hand out, Harry momentarily entertained the fantasy that he had just crossed over into "Brigadoon."

"Inspector Callahan?" she asked, hand still out, "I'm Sergeant McConnell, the cop you wouldn't let go on your arrest this morning."

Harry looked over the girl's shoulder at Devlin. Fatso stroked one forefinger over the other at his partner in a "shame-on-you" motion. Harry looked back at the girl's extremely pretty face, which was still stretched in an open smile fit to beat the band. He took her hand and shook it. It was warm, solid, and dry.

"You're the police woman from vice?" Harry marveled.

"Lynne McConnell, sergeant on the vice squad," she retorted. "Want to see my badge?" Fatso had a hard time holding back his laugh. He wound up snorting on the desk top.

"That won't be necessary," Harry said somewhat stiffly. He walked around his desk and pulled back on his chair. "Why don't you go wash windows or something?" he told Devlin.

"Right, Harry. Right," said Fatso, getting up quickly.

Harry sat down and motioned for the sergeant to do the same. She did, crossing her slim muscular legs and smiling pleasantly. "What can I do for you, Sergeant McConnell?" Harry asked, rifling through the top drawer on his desk.

"I think it is a matter of what I can do for you, Inspector," she replied easily.

"And what's that?" Harry asked just as easily, going from his top drawer to the first one on the right.

"I've been assigned to this case as the vice squad officer in charge," she explained with patience. "My job, no, my responsibility was to be with you this morning. I'm wondering why you wouldn't let me."

"I never," Harry began, then turned to Devlin, who was standing by. "Where's my cleaning kit?"

"Bottom drawer, Harry," Fatso said quickly. "I used it while you were with the captain. Sorry."

Harry pulled out the cleaning kit and dropped it on the desk. "I never said you could not go, Sergeant," Harry continued.

"No, Sergeant," Fatso took up, "all Harry said was, that given the situation, an extra officer from vice was not strictly necessary."

"My exact words," Harry overruled his partner, "were 'I don't want some girl from vice getting her ass shot off.' The aquarium was no place for an observer this morning."

The office got very quiet for a few seconds after that. McConnell's face had lost its smile. Instead she watched Harry very intently. Fatso stood back, trying to get into the next office by osmosis. Harry made the first new noise by standing, pulling off the dark suit jacket he had changed into, and hanging it on a wall hook. He then pulled out his Magnum, opened it, and started cleaning.

"Inspector Callahan," McConnell said carefully. "I have been on this case longer than you have. If it hadn't been for my department's work, you would have never known where to find those men. You would not have heard of The Professor. I think we had ... I had ... a right to be on the arrest."

"Sergeant McConnell," he answered, keeping his eyes on his weapon, "I don't doubt that you were instrumental in this arrest, and I do not deny that you had a perfect right to be there this morning. But I must add that if I had met you prior to the arrest, I would have been so concerned over your well-being that my own capability would have been severely handicapped."

This time the silence was stunned. Fatso looked at his partner as if he had sprouted wings. McConnell was completely disarmed. All the calm, rational answers she had been mentally preparing shot out through her scalp and into outer space. Suddenly she smiled warmly. Harry looked up from his gun, smiled back, and clicked it shut.

"Inspector Callahan," she asked, "what are you doing for lunch?"

"Sorry, Sergeant," said a new voice behind her chair,

"but Callahan is going to be busy." She turned to see Lieutenant Bressler stride in. "All hell's broken loose, Harry," he said. "You'd better come into my office. You too, Sergeant McConnell." Both officers got up.

"What about me?" Devlin asked.

"Go have lunch," Bressler instructed.

"Thank God!" said the starving cop.

"But don't leave the building," the lieutenant added.

Fatso's joy turned to resignation. "Great. Cafeteria franks 'n beans again."

"You eat that stuff," Harry told him as he pulled on his jacket and went out the door, "and you won't be sharing any squad car with me."

Bressler's office was different from all the other offices on the seventh floor in that it had a door that locked, its own ceiling, and a long leatherette couch. Both officers stood before the lieutenant's regulation desk as Bressler leaned on the back of his padded chair.

"Harry, you're off The Professor case," he said bluntly. "I'm sorry, but Captain Avery demanded it. I did my best, but you know Avery."

"Yeah," said Harry, who had been expecting it. It wasn't the first time he and the captain had had a similar conversation. And it probably wouldn't be the last.

"But what about the investigation?" McConnell inquired. "The Professor is still the head of the organization, and he's still at large."

"Your part of the investigation will continue," Bressler told her. "The captain commends you on your work so far. Only you'll be teamed with another set of homicide officers."

"But I'm so used to Inspector Callahan," McConnell said realistically. Harry glanced at her as Bressler looked down at his desk. She was grinning at him. When the lieutenant looked back up, both their expressions were back to normal.

"I'm sorry, Sergeant, but that's the way it is. You can go back to your department for the moment."

"Yes, sir," she said, turning to Harry. "It was a pleasure dealing with you, Inspector. I hope we can team up on another project some day." She held out her hand. Harry took it. They shook for the second time that morning. Harry nodded slightly. Both were well aware that she had chosen her words precisely.

McConnell then gracefully left. Harry unabashedly watched her go.

When the door had closed behind her, Bressler sat down with a heavy, wistful sigh.

"What is a girl like that doing on the vice squad?" Harry asked, turning to the desk.

"Driving everybody crazy," Bressler replied. "She's so damn angelic and earthy-looking, you don't know whether to give her some fatherly advise or attack her in the halls."

"She seems pretty sure of herself," Harry commented.

"Perfectly at peace," Bressler decided. "Knows what she's about and how good she looks. Can take care of herself, too. Top marks in self-defense and firearms. Dangerous combination."

"For who?" Harry wondered.

Bressler looked up. "What does that mean?"

"Skip it," Harry said, sitting on the couch. "What shit has hit which fan?"

"Fillmore District. Mission District. The headquarters of Uhuru."

"Oh Christ," said Harry. "Is that still around?"

"Still going strong, but quiet. Until now. What do you know about it?"

"It's a black liberation group," recalled Harry without much difficulty. "Big Ed Mohamid ran it. He was the guy who helped me out when the mayor was kidnapped by that People's Revolutionary Strike Force, and Captain McKay pegged Uhuru as the guys who did it."

"Yeah," Bressler said. "The 'Enforcer' case."

"Yeah," echoed Harry. "The one where Kate Moore got killed. Remember?"

"Yeah. Right. Sorry Harry. I should've figured you wouldn't have forgotten that."

Harry shrugged it off. "Anyway, I heard Mohamid kept a low profile after that. Started all sorts of charity programs and shit like that. Fed and clothed the poor.

Bought a ramshackle old Victorian house as a headquarters. What happened to all that?"

"Nothing," Bressler informed him. "It's all still there. But according to an anonymous phone tip we got this morning, only one thing has been added. A dead girl in the cellar."

Barbara Steinbrunner had died with her eyes open as well. They stared unblinkingly up at the coarse rafters and spotty insulation of the ceiling in the Uhuru cellar. She was completely naked with her hands tied to a pipe along one wall and each ankle tied, spread-eagled, to the base of an old, broken freezer. The coroner was going over her like a sculptor over a particularly rich piece of marble, the police photographer was circling around her like a flashing fly, and the uniformed men were discussing affably how such a good-looking girl could end up that badly. They weren't unduly shocked by her position. It wasn't anything they had not seen in a *Hustler* magazine.

"What's her name," Harry asked tiredly.

"I don't know," said Big Ed.

"How long has she been there?"

"I don't know."

"How did she get here?"

"I don't know."

"What's the capital of Nebraska?"

Without blinking an eye, Mohamid answered, "Lincoln."

Harry replied just as effortlessly. "Good. Now if anyone should ask, I'll be able to say I got some information out of you."

Nobody laughed, least of all Callahan or Mohamid. Both knew how serious the situation was. They sat opposite each other on milk-packing cases that were emblazoned on their sides with notices that read, "PROHIBITED FOR NON-DAIRY USE."

Next to them were the cellar stairs, upon which stood most of the house's Uhuru members. Harry looked up at them. They were different than the Uhurus Harry had encountered in the mid-seventies. They had wanted to

58

hold onto the spirit of revolution any way they could. They only succeeded in acting and dressing like assholes as well as alienating almost everyone they came into contact with.

Today, the dress was not unusual or garish, and the manner was more classically civilized. And there was no more burning hate in their eyes. Now, each one of the young black men and women on the stairs looked at Harry with a deep, smoldering dislike.

Harry stood up from his plastic perch and approached the coroner's assistant, lab man Walter White. Unlike his name, Walter was as dark-skinned as anyone on the stairs.

"Been taking notes?" Harry inquired.

"Every pearl of wisdom the M.E. grunts," White replied.

"What's new?"

"Body markings suggest that she suffered extremely painful physical and sexual abuse before she died. And she died about twelve hours ago."

"Any distinguishing marks? Anything linking her with this place?"

"Nothing yet," White reported. The lab man looked at the sullen crowd across the basement. "Doesn't look good, does it?"

"It stinks," answered Harry. "Reporters are already crawling all over the place, digging up meaningless shit from Mohamid's past, and this crowd already distrust the police so much they won't twitch an eyebrow to cooperate."

"Not after McKay tried to railroad them last time," White added. Both men fell silent. Walter examined the people on the steps. Harry studied the dead girl. "It just doesn't figure," muttered White.

"What doesn't figure?" Harry asked, turning.

"Look at her," White said, shrugging his head toward a black girl near the top of the stairs. Harry took a gander at a black girl attractive by any man's standards. Even though she was somewhat short and dressed simply in an old pair of jeans and a western shirt, she was still quite a slim, well-made package. "I mean, why go out and gang bang a white chick when you've got that in the house?" Walter wondered.

"I was wondering the same thing myself," mused Harry. "Delayed reaction black rage maybe?"

"This is the eighties, man," White retorted. "That don't wash no more, honky. It ain't 'burn, baby, burn' no more, bro, it's 'cash, flash, cash.' "

Harry snorted and turned back to the corpse in time to stare over the head of the coroner, who had just stepped up to him.

"I can't get anything more here, Harry," the doctor stated. "I'll have to go over her on the slab back at headquarters."

"All right," said Harry, waving the orderlies over, "untie her."

Just then Fatso Devlin came bustling in from the basement door that opened up on the tiny back yard, waving a sheet of paper.

"Got a positive I.D., Harry," he announced. "Her prints and picture matched up with someone at an anti-nuke demonstration arrest at Berkeley last year."

"Student?" Harry guessed.

"Student. Barbara Steinbrunner. Dropped out of classes two weeks ago. Teachers hadn't seen her since."

"Got a list of friends and known associates?"

"Teachers are working on that now."

"All right, let's get over to the campus," decided Callahan. "I'll give Bressler's fondest regards to Mohamid and meet you at the car."

Harry stepped around the hospital workers who were wrapping Barbara up for the one-way trip to the medical examiner's office and walked back to the milk case. Before he sat down he glanced up at the pretty black girl in the western shirt. High forehead, upturned top lip, terrific nose, and a no-nonsense body. Eighteen at the most, but definitely a woman to watch out for.

"Watch your ass," Harry told his ex-ally as way of introduction. "Take it easy and don't let any of your people overreact. This thing smells worse than a gay bar's bathroom, but it's not going to take much to set off a backlash in the community. Just don't plan any sudden trips to Rhodesia or burn down any municipal buildings, and I think it'll be OK."

Big Ed Mohamid looked up, his face expressionless. "Is that an order, sir?" he asked flatly.

Callahan lost all his humor. His eyes narrowed and he frowned. "Just some advise. Friend to friend."

"We were never friends," Mohamid stated.

Harry's reply was cut short by a commotion at the basement door. He turned to see Fatso struggling with a wiry young white man with curly hair waving a sheet of paper and shouting. Before Callahan could move, the thin guy slipped out of Devlin's grip and charged across the room at Mohamid.

Three black men swung down off the steps to land in front of Big Ed, effectively creating a human partition. The uniformed men started forward just as it seemed the curly-haired man would lay into Mohamid's guards. Harry stepped in front of the black trio, slapping one hand over the white guy's waving wrist and the other hand on the man's neck.

"Hold it!" the curly-haired white guy choked out. "Hold it!"

"It's a reporter," Devlin explained, trudging up to the tableau. "I couldn't stop him."

The reporter wrenched himself out of Harry's grip and pulled himself back together. "I just wanted to ask Mr. Mohamid about this letter he sent the newspapers," he said, pointing at the paper in his other hand.

"Letter?" Harry queried, looking at Big Ed from between two of his Uhuru members. Mohamid stared at the floor and didn't say anything. "What letter?"

"The one about how the revolution is still on and how whitey still had to pay," the reporter paraphrased quickly. "Do you have any comment, Mr. Mohamid?" he shouted under Harry's arm.

The three black men started forward as Harry grabbed the reporter under both arms and threw him into the clutches of two uniformed men. "Get him out of here," he ordered.

Fatso brought up the rear as the cops followed instructions. As soon as the cellar door closed behind them, Harry turned to Mohamid, who was standing among his reassuring Uhuru crowd.

"It's starting again," Mohamid intoned. "Get out, Callahan. Get out now."

Harry examined the group silently for a moment. All the men were standing tall, their faces expressionless but strong. The pretty girl was standing with them in the front, defiant, proud. They found dignity and pride in their unflinching dedication to each other. Their self-respect was replacing their common sense, Harry realized. Just as expressionlessly, the cop turned and walked out.

"Open and shut. Clear as day."

Fatso Devlin was going through his inventory of crime clichés as he drove toward the University of California campus at Berkeley.

"Easy as pie. Nothing to it."

"Either get on with your theory or shut the fuck up," Harry suggested from the passenger seat, one hand over his eyes.

"You're definitely losing your warmth and sensitivity, Harry," Devlin chortled as they passed over the San Francisco–Oakland Bay Bridge onto Route 80 north.

"What I'd like to lose is my warehouse of fat fuzz waiting to quip me to death every time I pull time with them."

"Don't you like me or Frank DiGeorgio?"

"If I don't get the fat guinea, I get the fat mick," Harry snarled. "Either way I lose."

"Now there's the tender sentimentalist I know and love," Devlin laughed.

"I wish DiGeorgio wasn't on vacation now," Harry continued seriously, looking out the window for the Telegraph Avenue exit. "He knew about the 'Enforcer' investigation."

"He ought to know," Devlin mentioned. "He's got a knife scar from his cock to his navel to prove it. Besides, what more do we need to know? Mohamid and his boys get a little hot, send a letter to the papers, get a little horny, and get caught with the corpse."

"He's not that stupid."

"Hey, Harry, no big deal. Everything goes fine until one of his boys gets a little queasy from all the gang-raping. He gets guilty, calls in a tip, and wham-bam-thank-you-ma'am, case closed."

"You keep talking like that," Harry warned. "And they're gonna promote you to captain."

The University of California at Berkeley was a solid West Coast establishment—laid back, spread open, and overpopulated. There were more than 20,000 students, many of them the glowing blond coeds that the Beach Boys and Sunkist Orange Soda commercials made famous. As the cop car pulled onto Bancroft Way, Harry marveled at the nearly stunning display of flesh in the early evening light. Tank tops, cutoffs, jogging shorts, swimsuits, elastic tube tops, slit skirts, designer jeans, high heels, roller skates, radios, leotards, boots, string bikini bras, and T-shirts of all kinds.

Ripped T-shirts, white T-shirts, net T-shirts, and T-shirts with such subtle messages emblazoned across the chests as "Good and Plenty," "Foxy Mama," "Mounds-Indescribably Delicious," "Lawyers Do it in Their Briefs," and "Stick in Your Tongue, You're Drooling on My Shirt." Occasionally these 100 percent cotton tops were stuck into shiny spandex pants. The main effect was that the cops had just died and gone to voyeur heaven. Harry remembered the times during the "Scorpio Sniper" case when he found himself looking in windows with binoculars during a stake-out and seeing the most interesting of things. The way things looked here, he wouldn't need the binoculars anymore.

"Find a place to park," Callahan instructed as the car slowed down in front of the Student Union. "I'll go in and try to find . . . ?"

"Hinkle," Devlin told him. "Roy Hinkle is . . . uh . . . was her counselor."

"Hinkle. Right." Harry pushed open the car door and hopped out without Fatso having to stop. He paused on the steps of the Union and looked down the street both ways. Down one direction he saw a variety of book stores. Down the other way he saw a long, squat building.

At the very edge of the building was the left side of a small shack. The rest of the dilapidated shed was masked by the building. Having gotten his bearings, Harry went inside.

The parade of feminine flesh continued unabated inside. There had to be mediocre women and men on the campus, but they were very hard to notice among the good-lookers. Almost everyone had something to show off and they were doing their best to spotlight their highlights. Harry made his way toward the Information desk slowly. He had had a hard life and a tough case to crack, but he still had eyes and he wasn't going to waste them.

One of those mediocre-looking women sat behind the long, light oak Information desk. Harry assured himself that she was probably a lovely, interesting girl once one got to know her, but somehow, all this seething skin exposure made his mind label the bodies around him merely "male" and "female" in self-defense. It was hard to see the flashing legs, tight bums, and wiggling tits stuffed inside all manner of clinging material as human beings. On display as they were, they just became so much meat.

"Roy Hinkle in this building?" Harry asked the girl.

"Mr. Hinkle?" the girl echoed, looking down at the typed list on her desk. "Let me see. Just a minute. . . ."

While she checked, Harry turned to scan the lobby again. In the corner a group of students were lounging around watching a six-foot-tall TV projection screen. They were watching the six o'clock local news. A studiedly serious woman reporter was gravely relating the murder of Barbara Steinbrunner while standing in front of the Uhuru house. By the looks of it, she wasn't the only reporter using Mohamid's headquarters as a rallying point. The students reacted to the report by reading the Berkeley *Barb*, talking to each other, picking their noses, and observing other television etiquette. On a campus of over 20,000 it wasn't likely that more than one person in every fifty knew each other.

Harry still couldn't understand why he was so pissed at their reaction, however. What did he want them to do?

Scream? Cry? Go running off in all directions? The damn thing was being reported on television—on the same channel that brought them *The Misadventures of Sheriff Lobo* and *Diff'rent Strokes*. Could he blame them for not taking it as reality? After all, what was he doing? Ogling at flaccid cheeks while a mediocre girl looked up Roy Hinkle.

"Here it is," said the girl, pulling Harry out of his fuzzy reverie. "It's Friday night, so Mr. Hinkle will be at his Independent Filmmakers' Spectrum series in the AV building."

Harry got directions and met Fatso on the Student Union steps. They walked by a few campus stores; each with copies of area newspapers as well as *Playboy, Penthouse, Oui, Forum, Hustler, Genesis, Variations, Chic,* and *Cosmopolitan* magazines displayed. There was a clothes store with a sale on Calvin Klein, Vidal Sasson, and Gloria Vanderbilt jeans. And there was a record store with such albums in the window as the latest one from Blondie, Carlene Cash, Tanya Tucker, Pat Benatar, and The Plasmatics. Devlin shook his head in wonder as they reached the Audio-Visual Building.

They followed directions downstairs into a long hallway with little windows near the top of the walls. They entered Room 27B. Inside was a cork-lined passage dotted by windows that revealed radio and video station setups. The only door open was one all the way down and to the left. Out of it was coming the weirdest noises. Harry and Fatso heard heavy breathing, tinkling sounds like a glass wind chime, and a light, feminine voice singing "La-la-la-la-la." That was followed by the sound of a small crowd giggling.

The pair approached the doorway and looked inside. Dozens of students were staring to the left in a dark room with a bluish glow all over them. Harry stuck his head farther into the room. To the left was a small screen. The kids were watching a strange movie. The glimpse Harry got was some huge close-ups of an eye, some piano keys, and the moving spools of a tape recorder.

"Where's Roy Hinkle?" he asked the first student in

front of him, a sandy-haired, vacuous-looking thin guy. The sandy-haired, vacuous-looking thin guy pointed back at the projector without taking his eyes from the screen. He was smiling all the while.

Harry rejoined his partner in the hall.

"What's going on?" Devlin asked.

"You got me," Callahan admitted. "Why don't you sit down and find out while I talk to Hinkle?"

"Oh, jeez, Harry," Fatso complained. "I can't stand this pseudo-intellectual modern age crap."

"Siddown," Harry repeated. "Broaden your horizons."

His fat partner found a seat near the front as Harry made his way to the projector. A hush had fallen on the audience as the film displayed a huge close-up of a phone. Harry wound up next to a blond man with full mustache and beard who was standing behind the 16mm projector, staring as intently at the screen as any of the students.

"Roy Hinkle?" Harry asked.

"Yes," the man said quietly. "Of course."

Harry ignored the tacked-on remark and pulled out his badge. "Inspector Callahan, Homicide department." He held his star near the side light of the projector.

"Oh!" Hinkle said in surprise. "Inspector. The police. Of course." He looked at the screen with regret. "And just at the good part, too," he clucked. "Well, no matter. Follow me, Inspector. We'll talk next door."

Hinkle left the film running and moved out into the hall. He led Harry to an office to the right of the 27B entrance. It was fairly small, with two typewriters, two phones, two desks, and a door between the pairs of everything. Hinkle pulled back one rolling chair and sat down as Harry pushed the mystery door open. Inside was a hall that connected every room on the right side. He stared down through the darkened video and radio spaces. Having relieved his curiosity, he returned his attention to Hinkle.

"Quite a place," he remarked to break the ice.

Hinkle didn't need the ice broken. His ice was permanently cracked. He liked to talk. "Oh yes," he said. "We have one of the finest collegiate facilities. The academic freedom it affords one is unparalleled."

"Unparalleled? Really?" Harry said lightly.

"Oh yes," Hinkle rattled on. "Take this course for instance. Independent Filmmakers' Spectrum. Every week a new film by a vastly underrated producer. Wes Craven, George Romero, and this week we have the Dario Argento film festival."

"Wes what?" Harry asked. "Dario who?"

"Argento, Argento," Hinkle lectured, his hands momentarily fluttering over his knees. "He's an Italian contemporary of Hitchcock whose stylized murder movies mask a satiric statement on the nature of politics in Italy today. He relates the psychological angst of the average Italian citizen in cinematic terms."

"What is he," Harry followed through in spite of himself, "a snuff film maker?"

"Inspector, Inspector," Hinkle admonished. "Where have you been? The big movie successes of the eighties have been murder movies. *Halloween, Friday the 13th, Mother's Day.* They've all been movies that existed only to kill off as many young people as possible in the most stylish way manageable."

Harry recalled seeing the commercials for these films now. He didn't remember individual spots, just a jumbled mélange of screaming women, running women, crying women, tortured women, knifed women, choked women, axed women, shot women, and raped women. The only other thing he recalled were a lot of bloody kitchen utensils.

"And you're showing those?" Harry asked incredulously. "Here? For college credit?"

"Well, of course!" Hinkle utilized the phrase for the third time. "You must understand, Inspector, that these films are probably the most accurate and anarchistic mirrors we have for today's society! They represent a release of frustration and a vicarious thrill. They're harmless . . . and they're funny."

"Funny?" Harry said slowly, his lip curling.

"Certainly. Look." Hinkle pivoted and switched on a small TV on the desk. Immediately a black and white picture of the screening room appeared with the audience watching the strange movie Harry had left Fatso with.

"We hooked up a video camera at the back of the room so the receptionist could see what was going on in class," Hinkle explained.

Harry leaned in to see a mature woman undressing for her bath. Her stripping was intercut with shots of a disguised figure, obviously the villain, creeping up to the house.

"Oh, this is the best part," Hinkle exclaimed. "This is Argento's *Deep Red,* the third in his series of truly masterful shock fests. *The Bird with the Crystal Plumage* was probably his most successful American film, but it had nothing on the likes of *Cat O'Nine Tails* and *Four Flies on Grey Velvet.* . . ."

"Mr. Hinkle," Harry interrupted, "what about Barbara Steinbrunner?"

"Barbara Steinbrunner? There was no Barbara Steinbrunner in *Deep Red.* Let's see, Suzy Kendall was in one, Mimsy Farmer was in another. . . ."

"Not in the movie, Mr. Hinkle," Harry said wearily. "In reality. Barbara Steinbrunner was one of your students who was found dead this morning."

"Oh yes!" Hinkle exclaimed without a trace of embarrassment. "Barbara. Pretty Barbara. Wonderful face. Very vulnerable."

"She's gone a bit beyond vulnerability, Hinkle," Harry said dangerously.

"Yes, of course, of course," Hinkle waved Harry's compassion away. "A very intriguing girl," he mused. "Not cold, exactly, not standoffish in as much as one could tell, but somehow she wouldn't let anyone get close to her. She kept even those who thought themselves her friends on a sort of 'arm's length intimacy.' It's like she already knew what she wanted and no one else fit in with her mental plan."

Harry was far from interested in Hinkle's psychological profile of the dead girl, so he tried to steer the foppish teacher onto more practical ground.

"Did she have any boyfriends? Anyone she went around with regularly?"

"Boyfriends? Barbara?" Hinkle responded, a disbelieving smirk on his face. "She had too many boyfriends and too few boyfriends, if you know what I mean."

Harry swore Hinkle was all set to lean in and wink. "No," Callahan answered. "I don't know what the hell you're talking about."

Hinkle's retort was interrupted by the moan of many voices coming from the little TV's speaker. The teacher turned and saw the students' heads turning around. The movie screen was blank. Harry spotted Devlin's face also looking questionably back at the projector.

"Oh, excuse me!" Hinkle said as he popped up out of the chair. "The second reel is over. I'll just put on the third and be right back."

Before Harry could say a word, Hinkle had shot out the door and down the hall. Harry stood alone in the front office for a few seconds before shaking his head and sitting down in the chair Hinkle had vacated. Great, he thought, watching the teacher's progress with the third reel on the tiny television set, his only contact with Steinbrunner's college life was a classic San Fran fruit. One thing Harry would bet on was that Hinkle didn't like Barbara for her body. Callahan hoped he didn't find him more attractive. It was tough enough talking to the teacher without fending off propositions. The cop waited patiently as the reel was finally secured and the film rolled again.

The movie had stopped at the worse possible time. The Italian woman was walking around her house, trying to locate a noise which had disturbed her. Finding nothing, she had gone back to her bath only to have the villain, in a slick overcoat, leather gloves, and slouch hat, run up behind her. That's where the second reel had stopped. The third reel took up where the villain smashed the woman's head against the bathroom tile and pushed her face into the scalding hot water of the bath. The camera was under the water so the audience could get a good view of the victim's face being scarred.

Harry turned away. If it wasn't for his heightened sensibility to fictional death, he would have become a dead body in reality. He was just in time to see a huge

69

black dude run in from the hall cradling a 4.85mm assault rifle. The cop's eyes bulged in amazement as his legs kicked themselves out from under him. His knees bent, his feet slapped up against the wall, and his back hit the tile floor as the room splattered inward, sprouting holes in the plaster above Callahan like a face of wildly exploding acne.

In seconds the automatic rifle had turned the cork walls and glass partition over the desk into confetti. The dust hadn't even begun to settle when the black monster jumped in through the open doorway. Harry had his Magnum out and shot him under the chin from his lying position on the floor. The guy's brain erupted from the front of his head like ash from Mount St. Helens. The red and grey goo spread out like a halo to do the beige ceiling with nauseous color.

Harry had no time to enjoy the modern art. Two more black killers came shouldering through the entrance. Harry flattened his heels against what was left of the bottom of the wall and pushed back with his legs. He slid backward across the tile floor toward the other hallway door. A line of bullets bore into the flooring after him, getting increasingly closer as he skimmed away. He tucked in his legs as his head hit the swinging barrier, and the bullets went by his toes and opened up a few holes near the bottom doorjamb.

Callahan had tumbled to his feet in the opposite hallway just as Devlin showed himself outside the screening room. He pulled out his snubnose .32, got one glimpse of the attackers' 4.85s as the black men turned toward him, shouted in surprise, and hurled himself backward as hard as he could. The entrance of the screening room spattered in every direction as Fatso slammed against a back row of students in folding chairs. His girth sent the first ten kids tumbling down like dominoes.

Harry moved into the next room in a crouch. It was the video center, filled with little orange TVs, movie cameras, and Betamaxes on black steel shelves. A bunch of installed television screens lined a window that opened into the hall where the black killers were. This glass partition seemed to become a TV as the black men

70

moved in front of it with their outlandishly modern weapons. They didn't wait to spot Harry, they just opened up on the room.

Glass shards and electrical wiring screamed in a steady shower all over the tiny cement enclosure as the assault rifles rasped out a low, steady grinding bark. Harry threw himself down, somersaulted, and came up against the wall between the video and the radio centers. As he tried to shield himself from the whirling glass and get a bead on the shooters, one black killer came racing around the corner from the office door Harry had escaped by.

The attacker let loose a stream of spinning lead just above Harry's head. Harry stared up into the bullet brook without blinking. These guys were not trying to aim at all. They figured let the 600 rounds a second do the work. Callahan blasted one round into the black man's face. He wasn't going to take a chance that the killer was wearing a bulletproof vest. What his move lacked in later ease of identification, it made up for in security.

The .44 slug ripped through the stream of machine-gun bullets, sending out a few sparks and two ripping-steel noises. This deflection slowed the .44 bullet down but that only made it worse for the black man when it hit. The lead splashed into his face nearly broadside, entering just under his nose, grinding up through his membranes, and lodging in his mind. The black man fell down, twitching.

Harry fell on his back just in case the last attacker was trying to box him in. He looked to his left and saw the back of the bastard's head through the glass of the radio station. He was bringing the assault rifle up to bear on Fatso and the room full of students.

The tall cop snapped off a shot from his prone position just to get the black's attention. The radio glass sprung a spider's web design, and the bullet cut off a tiny section of the man's Afro. It was enough. He spun around, screaming, turning the radio window into powder. Devlin took the opportunity to shoot him in the back. That only got the big black man more upset. He screamed, whirling back to the glass room and falling against the wall, his head below the broken partition.

What Harry couldn't see, he could rarely shoot. In

71

addition, he couldn't be sure that his slug could get through the wall where he thought the last black man was crouching. But he couldn't let Devlin fight off the maddened, wounded killer alone. Harry needed another weapon in the split second he had before the killer opened up on the room full of students. From his position on the floor the only thing in reach that wasn't bolted down was a large microphone on a multijointed metal stand. The stand was bent in such a way that it hung down near a disc jockey's face and the disc jockey could pull it closer to his mouth. Harry kicked it over.

Normally the big mike would bounce off against the radio window, but the radio window was no more so the heavy microphone fell out and down. Harry heard the surprised yell of the black and saw the barking bullets of his 4.85mm tear a circle in the screening room ceiling. Before the last cartridge clattered on the hall tile, Callahan was on his feet. He pushed his Magnum barrel out the open partition, rammed it against the top of the black man's head and pulled the trigger. This man's mind came through his mouth.

Harry only regretted that it wasn't a cleaner death. He got no satisfaction out of presenting the film class with a man puking out his own brains, but he couldn't afford to deal with any "freeze" or "hold it" lines. When a team of big guys come running into a college class with assault rifles, no one could count on them giving up even when they were caught dead to rights. Whether they were terrorists intent on holding the class hostage or assassins intent on turning Callahan into Wheatena, it wasn't exactly the M.O. of rational pros.

Harry was taking off his dark suit jacket to cover the gore when the vacuous-looking student appeared in the doorway, staring at the gruesome corpse with wide eyes.

"Hey, neat," the student said.

Harry dropped his jacket over the body anyway. He brushed by the vacuous-looking kid to collect Devlin. He was just in time for the end of *Deep Red*. It turns out that the mother of the boy everyone suspected was the real murderer, and she gets hers, while trying to open David Hemmings up with a meat cleaver, by catching her large pendant in the door of a rising elevator. The chain tightens around her neck, and her head gets ripped off. The end credits roll over a deep, red pool of blood on the elevator floor.

Harry had to hand it to the independent producers. They always made it with the happy endings.

Chapter Four

If the case had gone to a higher court, somehow the defense attorney would have made it all Rose Ray's fault. It was the bright red wrap dress, he might proclaim, setting her out like a beacon in the dim Fillmore streets. It was the dark blue T-strap shoes with the beige high heels, he might add, marking her as a haughty bitch who had nothing better to do than entice and excite every person she came into contact with.

Then the defense would blame her for not drinking Drano and grinding a broken bottle on her face to lessen her attractiveness. Why, by not wearing a burlap bag and bathing regularly in hydrochloric acid, she was just asking for trouble. And Rose Ray got it.

If the truth be known, her natural beauty was not the deciding factor in her fate, although it helped mightily. If Harry Callahan thought the five-foot-two-inch black girl on the steps of the Uhuru cellar was good looking in jeans and a shirt, he should've seen her in the dress and heels. Her mound of loosely curled black hair surrounded her well-shaped face like a glow. Her facial beauty was further heightened by the rouge on her cheeks and lips. She handled the highlighting gracefully, giving the impression that she wore no makeup at all.

The thing that really did her in was her location and family background. Her only real family was Uhuru, and she was heading back there after a date. She was heading back on an empty street that was supposedly dangerous only for white people. Rose Ray was about to find out differently.

Naturally, it had to happen fast. Rose walked past the mouth of an alleyway. She was walking the way she had always been told; right down the middle of the sidewalk —never too close to either the buildings or the street. In this case, her teachings didn't help her at all.

Two men took one long step out of the dark mouth of the alley and they had her. Rose had occasionally fantasized about this happening. It was hard to live in the area of town that she did and not think about it. But when she daydreamed she had always figured that if they didn't kill her instantaneously she could fight and make enough noise to get away. Only she was fantasizing about maddened rapists. The men who took her were professional.

The first one slapped his hands on the top of her head and under her chin. He pushed while the other man stretched a dark, wet band of something across the lower half of her face, just below her nose. The thing was put on her mouth like a big Band-Aid. The man peeled something off both sides as it adhered to her skin. She was caught by surprise. Her body bent backward, and she nearly fell. By the time she found her footing again, both pairs of hands were off her, her mouth was tightly closed, and she felt the moisture around her lips dry and harden.

She was still somewhat off balance when her hands started to move toward her face. Halfway there, the four hands of her assailants smacked into her back and propelled her toward the side of a van parked at the curb. Her hands went out in front of her to serve as protection against the metal vehicle, but just before she seemed to hit the side, it slid away, and she fell into two more pairs of waiting hands. They wrapped around her torso and pulled her all the way in as the two original assailants hopped in the back, pulling the door closed after them.

Rose was dropped on her back, her head nearest the rear of the van, her feet pointing toward the front windshield. She couldn't see the dashboard because a curtain separated the cab from the back. Hands were firmly holding her elbows and knees to the carpeted floor. Her mind told her mouth to open and shout but her lips wouldn't respond. Her brain demanded her mouth to open, but when the muscles attempted to react she felt sharp, needling pain. It was the pain of trying to pull your tongue off dry ice. Her lips were sealed together as if she had kissed cement.

She began to hum in panic. The hands on her arms remained sure, but she managed to pull one of her legs out from under the grip. She kicked out at the van walls, only to feel her toe hit something soft. It made the sound of a penny hitting a bed. Her only accomplishment was to expose her handsome leg from the skirt of her wraparound dress. Her attackers hardly seemed interested. While one hand retrieved her loose leg, another hand began massaging the side of her neck.

"Don't fight it," she heard a gentle male voice admonish. "We won't hurt you. Just relax and take it easy. There's nothing to worry about. Just keep still and you won't come to any harm."

The words sent a chill up her spine. She couldn't just lie there, she had to fight. But try as she might, her limbs wouldn't respond. She felt her eyes rapidly blinking and the warmth of the hand on her neck. She wanted to see the faces of the people holding her down, but her eyesight was getting fuzzy. She groaned in despair as she felt herself drifting down to a dark, soft cloud.

"There, there," she heard the male voice from far, far away. "That's better, isn't it? Isn't that nice?"

Rose Ray didn't lose consciousness. She floated in a tender, silky world inside her head. She felt too weak to do anything but feel. The activity around her body in the van, meanwhile, had picked up speed.

One of the men who had pushed her in jumped on the

driver's seat and propelled the vehicle to an alley three blocks away. On the way there, the van passed the Uhuru house. They had to make their careful way around several news trucks and a small bunch of reporters, but since the van only had two curtained windows in the back besides the cab's glass, no one was the wiser. And the driver couldn't resist throwing a sarcastic wave at the front porch.

The alley was big enough to hold the van and the large Cadillac which had pulled alongside. Four black men sat silently in the parked Caddy. Inside the van they were taking off Rose Ray's clothes. The quartet of kidnappers in the back moved her around like a flaccid Barbie Doll. Occasionally her eyelids would open, but her dark eyes saw nothing. Occasionally she would moan behind the thin seal over her mouth, but the sound was no greater than a sigh.

The red wrap skirt came off to reveal a dark blue spandex bra and panties. A knife suddenly appeared in a man's hand. He sliced open the bra between her breasts and over both shoulders. The garment fell away.

"Good," said a feminine voice. "Size 34 and sturdy."

While two men sat Rose up and held her arms above her head, the other two men pulled off her shoes and quickly measured her waist and inseam. Incongruously, one man then measured her shoe size. And while they toiled, a woman was meticulously wrapping tape tightly around the black girl's chest.

The men working below her waist moved over to a small box against the van wall. Out of it they pulled a dark, man's shirt, a cap, a pair of sneakers, and some straight-leg jeans. They laid the jeans out on the floor next to Rose. One man used a needle to punch a small hole behind the knee of the right denim leg, then punched a hole above the knee of the left pant leg. The other man picked at a special flap of cloth just under the jean's waistband to reveal a zipper alongside both pockets. He then unzipped both pockets so they opened like doors on either side of the pants.

By then the woman had finished taping down Rose's

breasts. The tape had pressed them out against her chest, not flattening her, but greatly diminishing her femininity. As the woman cut away the last piece of sticky stuff, a man strapped a pad across her stomach, evening out the torso girth somewhat. The dark shirt was passed over and put on the woozy girl. When it had been buttoned down the front, she looked several inches wider—almost mannish.

She was laid back down, stomach up, as the men nearest her feet pulled out a roll of thick, rubber-coated wire. They tied a loop around both her wrists, then tied those to both her thighs. The woman then taped the rest of her hands flat against the side of her thighs. The men tied a double loop of wire just above her right knee, letting a double strand hang down off it.

Then the jeans were pulled on. When they got to her knees, a man pushed the two hanging ends of the wire through the hole in the pant leg. He then pushed it through the other hole in the top of the other leg. Before the jeans were pulled up any higher, he tied the long double strand tightly around Rose's left leg, just above her left knee. He pulled it tight so one leg was above the other. Finally he pulled the jeans all the way up. The pockets zipped back over her bound hands so none of the wire or tape showed. They tucked the shirttail in and sat Rose up again.

The woman went to work on her hair while one man held her head still and another man took out a makeup kit and approached her face. The woman pinned the loose curls back while the man smeared her face with a uniform base color. He was careful to blend the edges of the dark tape in with the rest of her skin. Then, taking out a delicate brush and some pots of color, he began drawing over the seal on her mouth.

Rose Ray awoke completely in the back seat of the Cadillac. She turned her head to the left. A black man smiled at her. She looked forward, her vision clearing. Two more black men in the front seat were turning around and smiling. She looked down at someone else's body. An unobtrusive seat belt held a man's waist firmly against the plush seat. The man's knees were folded over each other. As much as she tried, Rose couldn't get these alien legs to uncross.

The Caddy was a mediumly expensive one so there wasn't much leg room. It kept her from kicking out with the bottom of these strange legs. On her feet were high-rise sneakers. Her hands were in the pant pockets. She couldn't pull them out. She couldn't even wiggle her fingers. She looked to the right. A tall woman with streaked brown hair and loop earrings stared back at her and smiled.

"I see you're ready to go," the woman said. "We just couldn't drive off with you lying against one of your friends here. That would defeat the whole purpose of the exercise."

Rose tried to reply, but no sound came out and the stabbing, rending pain came back.

"No, no, dear," the woman cautioned. "Be quiet. Your lips are sealed by a plaster-chloroform mixture. Just enough chloroform to keep you weak but not enough to affect those near you. And more than enough plaster to serve. Only we have another mixture to get it off your face. If you tried, all your skin would be ripped off with it."

The woman placed her hands on Rose's arm and shoulder and moved her against the man to her left. "So just sit up straight, dear. It would be too dangerous to move you to your destination all bound up in the back of a van. It would look too suspicious when Mohamid finds you missing. We're going to get you out of the district right before their eyes. And they won't even see you."

To prove her point, the woman reached into her large pocketbook and pulled out a mirror. She held it before Rose. Someone else's face stared back. Her hair had been pushed under a cap and the back had been cut off to a boyish style. Her skin was a darker color. And worst of all, there were a pair of dark, male lips painted exactly where her full, rosy lips should be. To anyone looking in the car there would be just three black guys in the back seat, one with his hands nonchalantly in his pockets.

Rose's face crumbled and tears welled up in her eyes as she looked in supplication at the woman.

"Ah, now for the final touch," the woman remarked as she put the mirror back in her purse. When her hand came out, it was holding two cotton balls. "Close your eyes," she instructed. Rose pulled herself back, her eyes widening with fear. "Close your eyes," the woman said again, quieter. Rose felt a male hand on the back of her head. She closed her eyes.

The woman placed one specially treated cotton ball each over her eyes. They stuck her lids closed and also absorbed any moisture that leaked out. The woman then pulled a large set of sunglasses out of her bag. With a flourish, she placed them over Rose's eyes.

"We're all set then," she concluded, stepped out of the Caddy and waved a black man holding the door for her in. "Have a nice ride," she breathed to Rose. The frightened black girl felt the two men on either side of her press in. One put his arm around her shoulders.

"Act naturally," he warned. "A sudden move and you'll never see how you died."

Rose sobbed silently, drily, as the car drove out of the alley and into the night.

It was Saturday afternoon and ABC-TV was waving a tit in Harry Callahan's face. The cop was recuperating from yesterday's classroom attack by re-creating the dream of every red-blooded American male. That is, he was sitting around in his apartment, wearing an undershirt, drinking beer, and watching a football game. The only thing marring this classically macho tableau was that Harry was fifteen minutes early. The pre-game show was not set to commence until 1:30. So Harry was stuck with the last quarter of *American Bandstand*.

Dick Clarke was there, looking about the same as he had for the past three decades, and the set was more or less as Harry remembered it from his teens, but the dancers were completely different. Harry couldn't help but marvel at the teens and cameramen's almost total lack of taste and innocence. These kids didn't want to dance, they wanted to shake whatever they had the most of, and the photographers wanted a close-up of whatever that was.

Harry stared in quiet awe at the bouncing breasts of young girls dissolving into high-heel, ankle-strap stiletto shoes dissolving into thrusting pelvises dissolving into heavily painted faces winking and licking their lips. Harry had to get another beer after a cameraman shot from the floor up a girl's dress as she spun around in place. Whatever happened to the freshness of Kenny Rossi and Carol Ann Scaldeferri and Frankie Lobis and Arlene Sullivan, he wondered, and the other regular dancers on "AB's" golden age twenty-five years ago?

The telephone rang in reply. That was the only answer he was going to get for the moment. Lieutenant Bressler was on the other end of the line, and he wasn't interested in pubescent flesh.

"Harry, get down to Uhuru headquarters," he demanded without so much as a hello. "All hell has broken loose."

"What's the matter?" Harry wanted to know.

"I don't know," cried the lieutenant, "but for some reason, Mohamid boarded up all the entrances and opened fire on the reporters."

"Opened fire?"

"Guns, Callahan! Weapons. The Uhuru headquarters has become an armed camp!"

When Harry got to the Mission District, things were already in full swing. An impressive police cordon was around the Victorian house, and cops were coming out of the woodwork in every dwelling nearby. There were snipers on the roofs across the way, SWAT teams crawling all over the trees, and a platoon of uniformed men behind a fleet of squad cars lining every street on four sides of the Uhuru house.

Mohamid's place was tightly closed with planks nailed to the inside of the windows and not a soul was to be seen in the yard or garage. For the present, all guns were silent. The area birds and assorted wildlife were taking the opportunity to sing and buzz their heads off, as if absolutely nothing was happening that sunny San Francisco afternoon.

Harry was waved over by a uniformed man. He flashed the cop his badge as he got out and asked where Captain Avery was. Callahan was sent over to the captain, who was holding court behind his big Cutlass Supreme, which was parked in the front yard of the house across from the Uhuru residence.

When Avery saw Harry approaching, he sent the collected officers on their way. He turned to greet Callahan full front, with a satisfied smile on his face.

"Still think Mohamid is an innocent dupe of a frame-up, Callahan?" the captain barked.

"Maybe," Harry said slowly, deliberately. "What happened?"

"Nothing!" Avery proclaimed. "Everything was exactly as it was. People were coming and going, when, suddenly, for no reason at all, Mohamid shuts the place up and starts firing upon the police guards and members of the press."

Harry ignored Avery's dramatic rhetoric for the most part. His flowery regular conversation was born of years facing those very same members of the press. "For no reason at all?" Harry repeated. "Did anyone ask Mohamid?"

"No one can get near Mohamid!" Avery declared. "If anyone goes near the place they're shot at."

"From where?"

"Everywhere."

"Did you actually see a shot from every single window," Harry asked purposefully, "or are you guessing?"

Avery bristled at that, drawing himself up to his full height, which was still two inches shorter than Harry. "Might I remind you, Inspector, that I'm the captain and not the other way around?"

"No, that's OK," said Harry, squinting across the street at the silent Uhuru home. "Don't go out of your way."

"I won't stand for any more of your insubordination, Inspector!" Avery shouted in Harry's ear. "I only had you called here to show you how wrong you can be. If you had arrested Mohamid when we found the Steinbrunner girl, none of this would have happened!"

"How do you figure?" Harry asked, looking down at the captain's flushed face.

"Mohamid knew you'd do some more investigating, so he sent three of his men to kill you at the university."

"What for?" Harry interrupted.

"So you wouldn't find the link between him and the girl," Avery contended.

"What link?"

"The link we are sure to find if we look hard enough," Avery maintained. "And when he failed to kill you, he decided to make a stand here."

"I don't understand," Harry said flatly. "If he was guilty, why not just make a run for it?"

"These aren't rational people!" Avery exclaimed. "These are people who'd kidnap, gang-rape, and murder a beautiful blond girl!"

Avery looked up at Callahan in triumph, as if his logic was unimpeachable. Harry looked down, pasting an expression that said "Why didn't *I* think of that" on his face. He waited until after the captain had turned to face the Uhuru house to shake and hit the side of his head as if there were water in his ear.

"Hand me that megaphone," Avery told a subordinate. "I'm going to give Mohamid an ultimatum."

"Uh, excuse me, Captain," Harry said as the bullhorn was handed up to his blond boss. "But may I try to talk to Mohamid before we do anything final?"

Avery smiled at the inspector. "Know when to admit your mistakes, eh, Callahan?" he smirked. Harry looked at him through narrowed lids, as if the sun were in his eyes. His top lip curled up. "Well," Avery continued, "you two go back a ways." He handed Harry the megaphone. "Go ahead. Give it a shot."

Callahan took the device and walked slowly toward the picket fence around the Victorian. He stopped when the top of the barrier touched his thighs. The rest of the cops watched and waited. The tension in the air was thick enough to cut.

"Mohamid," Harry called through the speaker. "This

84

is Harry Callahan. I don't know what's the matter, but this is only making it worse. You know you're not going to get out of this alive the way things are. If you force them these guys will rip you up like so much paper. I don't care how many guns you have or how many men you have. I don't care if you have a box of grenades in there. There'll be no fighting your way out.

"A couple of guys might die out here, maybe, but all you guys will die in there for sure. You start it ... you even look like you're *gonna* start it and these boys will be ready to send you to hell. And if you think that's going to make you a martyr to the cause, forget it. All these reporters out here will be happy to film every second of the destruction in slow motion and from twelve angles and it won't change a goddamn thing. They'll put it on the six o'clock news tonight, and nobody'll give a shit. You'll be sandwiched between a Charmin commercial and a report about talking parrots and none of your brothers or sisters will even care."

Harry lowered the bullhorn for a second, licked his lips, and went back to it. "I'm going to come in now, Big Ed. I'm going to walk to the front door and get in any way I can. I would appreciate it if you would meet me there. I give you my personal guarantee of protection."

Harry handed the megaphone to the cop nearest him. The cop scurried from the cover of his squad car's fender, grabbed the horn, and scurried back. Harry turned. Captain Avery was shaking his head furiously and mouthing the word "No." Harry turned back to the house and stepped over the picket fence.

He zipped open his cordoroy jacket as he started the long walk to the front steps. He felt the reassuring weight of his Magnum in its shoulder holster as well as the three auto-loaders in his jacket pocket. He saw a variety of details on the house that he hadn't noticed before. The porch was built from a wooden frame that seemed to attach itself to the front of the place. On either side of the stairs was balsa-wood crosshatching.

The thick wooden front door was flanked by two medium-sized picture windows consisting of a large central pane and four thinner, smaller, rectangular ones. Above that was the porch ceiling. Above the porch roof were three more regularly sized windows and above that were two gable windows, both made of stained glass.

Harry made it to the first step. He looked to his left and right. Cops, cops, uniformed and plainclothed behind marked and unmarked cars, as far as the eye seemed to see. Harry made it to the second step. Nothing happened. The silence was deafening and other clichés of that type. Harry's shoe descended on the third step. Only one more step and a porch that seemed as long as a football field to go. Harry made it to the fourth step.

He was bringing himself onto the porch when it happened. The simple wood mailbox nailed to the porch column next to Harry's head exploded into several pieces.

Harry fell down, instinctively throwing his body to the least exposed area. He fell backward and to the side, hitting the grass to the left of the Uhuru house stairs. The world blew up above him. The simultaneous tightening of so many trigger fingers made a sound that was extremely impressive. The crash of those bullets hitting anything they were pointed at was also humbling. Harry resisted putting his palms over his ears. Instead, he dragged out his .44 and rolled toward the crosshatching of the porch.

The world continued to sound like an acid rock and roll band as his back slapped the side of the porch. He looked up to see whole hunks of the porch's floor go spinning off into the yard. It wouldn't be long before someone hit him, either accidentally or otherwise. Harry pushed himself as hard as he could against the balsawood barrier.

The thin planks gave way, and Callahan was rolling across the dirt under the porch. Little spotlights of sunshine reached from the flooring to the ground, thanks to bullet holes. Harry stopped to look out the hole he had made in the wall section of the porch setup. None of the front-line cops seemed to be paying any attention to him at all. He took the moment to collect his thoughts.

Where had that first bullet come from? Harry remembered seeing it rip apart out the corner of his eye. He remembered unconsciously listening for the weapon's report to sound from either inside the house or in the rank and file of the police platoon. He remembered not hearing a report. Any bullet powerful enough to smash that mailbox had to make a noise . . . unless it was silenced. And why would anyone want to use a silenced high-powered weapon?

Harry scowled deeply and with feeling. The signs of conspiracy were creeping all over the Uhuru house like ivy. But to prove anything, Harry had to get out of his present predicament.

Rolling over so that he faced the house wall, he saw a small cellar window near the ground. Sure enough, his impression that the porch had been attached whole to the house now seemed to be correct. There was a basement window beneath the wooden structure. Harry straightened himself out and crawled the remaining distance. The glass was caked over with years of grime, but Harry could see through it enough to note that no one was around. He grabbed ahold of the frame and pulled. With a nasty creak, it gave way.

Harry didn't stand on ceremony. He immediately pulled it all the way open and tumbled through. He slid down the rough rock wall a few feet and landed on the concrete floor. Across the basement, one young black man was guarding the door to the back yard. He wasn't expecting a cop to roll out from under the porch, so he wasn't fast enough. By the time he had started to bring his army surplus rifle around, Harry was pointing the Magnum at his head.

"It would be a shame to splatter that fine Afro all over the place," Harry said softly. "Why don't you put the gun down so I don't have to."

The boy entertained the notion of giving up his life for Uhuru, but then he looked down the .44 barrel and saw his maker in Cinerama. The rifle went down very fast, and the hands went up.

Harry walked across the cellar, placing the Magnum barrel on the boy's forehead. He looked disdainfully at the rifle. "Hungarian sniper rifle," Callahan commented, "circa 1943." Then he hit the boy in the jaw with a sharp left. The black kid's head snapped back and hit the cellar door frame. The combination of the two blows was enough to put him out for the duration of the day.

Harry didn't wait for the kid to crumble to the floor. He was already jumping up the basement steps three at a time. He slowed only when he neared the door at the top. He wondered whether he should wait in relative safety until it was all over or risk entering a house he knew almost nothing about, filled with rabid young militants armed to the teeth. Then he pictured Captain Avery's face. Harry opened the door.

Immediately three bullets bashed their way through the wood from the other side and slapped into the sloping concrete above Harry's head. All thought of a cautious approach fled from Harry's thinking. He ducked, swung himself forward, hit the door with his shoulder, and catapulted into the kitchen. He came up in a crouch with his gun ready.

The room was empty. The bullet trio had come through the windows from outside. Harry kept down as he moved toward the adjoining room. The chatter of weapon fire remained constant as he steeled himself for entry into the dining room. From his position low to the floor he saw one and a half black backs through the doorway. They, too, were crouched, aiming fairly ancient rifles out breaks in the window boarding.

Harry put a loose plan of action together. As he remembered from being led to the Steinbrunner corpse in the cellar, the dining room adjoined the living room, which had a staircase leading up. Harry's brilliantly incisive plan was to somehow get to that stairway alive. It was the best he could do under the circumstances.

Also, given the situation, Callahan didn't want to unduly surprise his unknowing hosts. In their state they'd cut him down as a panicky afterthought. So instead of marching or charging into the dining room, Harry continued his crouching crabwalk.

The dining room was a mess. Tables were overturned. All the glasses were broken. The chairs looked like a giant cat had exercised his claws on them, and the wall looked like a connect-the-dots game in a children's book.

Harry could not clearly recall what had been caused by the shoot-out and what was the way Uhuru normally lived.

His entrance did not go unnoticed. As soon as he moved in, he saw a Uhuru member to his left, hiding behind an overturned easy chair. The guy had a .22 Saturday Night Special clutched in his hands, which was no good for the long-range fight but perfectly suitable to cause Callahan some internal damage. Still not wanting to take anyone else's attention away from the torrent of cop bullets that was perforating the place, Harry leaped atop the chair, catching the black man's gun wrist in one hand and swinging the barrel of the .44 across his scalp. The man screamed in pain so Harry hit him again, coming down with the Magnum butt right in the middle of his head.

He stayed quiet, but his previous scream had been enough. Harry looked over as one of the men by the window saw him. The man turned completely around and leaped to his feet, his rifle coming up on a level with Harry's chest at the same time.

Harry threw himself off the chair and swung his own gun around just as a cop bullet sizzled in from outside and drove halfway through the standing Uhuru's back. The black man fell face first flat on the floor, the heavy rifle clattering next to him, unfired.

That got the other men to turn around, but they were smart enough not to get up. Harry saw his chance, so he rolled to his feet and ran as fast as he could backward into the living room.

Pieces of the wall ripped off after him. Whether it was the Uhuru's shooting or more police lead he never found out. He slipped on some broken crockery on the floor, stepped on an outstretched hand, and slammed into the closet door next to the stairway. He turned around, dazed, as Uhurus across the living room saw him and brought their guns to bear.

Harry was framed in the entrance to the stairs as a veritable firing squad blasted at him. The closet door, the tattered rug between his feet and the walls were peppered by the shots, sending Callahan back and down. He fired his own gun once between his outstretched legs, then scrambled over a landing and around a corner.

He stood up on the stairs as a wild-eyed Uhuru came roaring down. The black man stopped five steps up from Harry and tried to bring his rifle around. Harry fell forward, grabbed the guy's ankle, and pulled. The man slipped and fell heavily backward, bashing his head on the second landing. Harry ran up, grabbed the rifle from the wounded man's hands, and used it like a golf club to send the Uhuru cartwheeling the rest of the way down.

Harry raced around the second stairway corner to three more steps and a thin hall leading to four rooms. Light was streaming in a destroyed window frame at the other end of the hall. Figures would dart in and out of this light flood like ghosts, racing from one room to another. The accumulated heat was so great that steam seemed to be rising from the floorboards.

Two Uhurus from the nearest room ran out toward the stairs. Just as they saw the cop, Harry buried the rifle butt in the face of one and shot the other in the stomach. The hit one fell backward like a board and the shot one spun back into the room he came from.

Harry didn't wait for reinforcements. He raced up the last three steps and charged down the hallway. He had passed two of the rooms on the floor when a big black man, bald as a billiard ball, slammed into him from the side. Harry saw an army .45 in his hand so he grabbed it. He felt the other man do the same with his .44 wrist.

They spun farther down the hall, slamming against the walls as they went. Their faces were no more than three inches away from each other as they struggled. The Uhuru tried to knee Callahan in the balls. Harry blocked it with one leg and tried to keep the black man's back facing the broken window at all times.

The bald man screamed in frustrated rage and shot off his .45. The gun sounded unnaturally loud in the enclosed space and seemed to bring a flurry of new police activity through the window. A bullet ground a hole in the wall next to Harry's nose. He heard another shot thunk into the black man's leg. The Uhuru shouted again. Harry threw all his weight forward. The two crashed down into the corner, Harry on top.

The cop wrenched himself from the bald man's grip and stood. The wounded Uhuru kept shouting and tried to sit up and aim his .45 at the same time. Harry tromped on the man's neck. The shouting stopped and the man went down for good. Harry spun, seeing another stairway at the end of the hall just as another Uhuru ran out of the fourth room. Before the man could react, Harry grabbed the barrel of his rifle, spun him around toward the window, and kicked him as hard as he could in the stomach. The Uhuru flew backward out of what was left of the dormer.

Harry didn't stay to watch the man dive backward down, smash face first into an abutment, and land on his side in the yard. He was up the second stairway as fast as he could go. The light was much less there, and there were only two doorways cut out of the sloping roof line. There was a small landing between these two doors upon which another Uhuru was waiting. He didn't blast Harry as soon as he showed because he wasn't expecting a white cop yet. By the time he brought his gun to bear, Harry had swiped it aside with his gun hand and smashed the Uhuru as hard as possible in the face.

The black man stumbled back, his nose a crushed and bloody mess, but he didn't go down. He fired his gun into the floor. Harry saw the bullet hit between two rafters off the landing. The lead went right through. Harry realized that the attic consisted only of these two rooms and the small landing. All the rest was insulated rafters. Harry threw subtlety to the wind and leaped into the air. He grabbed one sloping roof rafter in each his hands, swung, and kicked the last Uhuru in the chest with both feet.

The black man flew backward off the landing, landed on the orange padding between two horizontal ceiling rafters and kept going. He slammed into the ceiling of the second floor and crashed through. In a shower of plaster, concrete and insulation, he smashed into two of his brothers in the first room next to the staircase.

Harry kicked open the door to his left. The room was empty. He heard steps on the stairway. He shot down it without looking. He rammed the right doorway with his shoulder. It broke open, Harry fell and rolled. He came up with his Magnum pointed between Big Ed Mohamid's eyes.

The tiny attic room was like an oven. The only opening to the outside was a small stained-glass window, and no one was about to open that. Big Ed sat on a crate in the corner farthest away from the window. His eyes were downcast, and he was unarmed. His sweaty black face was colored in blues, greens, and reds. He looked calmly at Harry's Magnum.

Three black men charged into the room. They stopped when they saw Callahan's target. Harry looked at them, then returned his gaze to Mohamid.

"Leave us," Mohamid told his men.

"But," said a nervous one, "the cops . . . they're all around us. . . !"

"Leave us!" Mohamid demanded. The men slowly, reluctantly, left. They closed the door after them.

The noise of the bullets sounded very far away now. Harry felt like he had entered a mausoleum of a patriarch not yet dead. The atmosphere was stifling, the room was claustrophobic, the smell was nauseating, and the place was bathed with otherworldly colors.

Mohamid ignored the gun in front of his face. He looked back down and frowned.

"Nothing has changed," he said, his voice empty in the strange place.

"Now is not the time to discuss it," Harry said. "Men are being killed downstairs."

"How could I stop it?" Mohamid asked.

"Give up," Harry seethed. "Surrender."

"They would kill us anyway," Mohamid said sadly. "That's why they're here."

"What are you talking about?" Harry demanded. "What am I doing here, then?"

"Committing suicide," Mohamid decided. "We did not fire the first shot."

"Neither did they," Harry revealed. "Someone's playing us both for assholes."

Big Ed Mohamid looked up then, a dawning light in the back of his black eyes. "You know, then?"

Callahan pushed his .44 back into its shoulder holster under the scuffed jacket. "I know something's definitely fucked, and we're both doing our best cunt impersonations."

"I didn't think anyone would believe me," Mohamid marveled.

"No one will," Harry said. "But me. If you want something done about it, though, you've got to stop this mess."

Mohamid seemed about to agree when the smoke began curling from under the door. It was a thick white smoke intermingled with curls of black. It certainly wasn't more steam heat.

"Ah shit," Harry said. "The place is on fire. Is there any other way out of here?"

"No," Mohamid said.

"Come on," said Harry, hauling Big Ed up by the arm. Callahan pushed him toward the door. Mohamid got it open, and the pair stood on the landing with smoke and little licks of flame belching out from the hole in the second floor ceiling.

"It's coming from the front," Mohamid realized.

"And any second that insulation is going to blow or start giving off poison fumes," Harry shouted, already pounding down the back stairs. "Move it!"

The Uhuru leader ran down after Harry, and the two turned the corner at the bottom to face a wall of crackling yellow. Mohamid started coughing on the back of Harry's neck.

"Miserable fuckers probably didn't take time off from target practice to call the fire department," Harry growled, trying to spot a way out.

"Out the window!" Mohamid yelled above the roar of the flames, pointing to the opening Harry had kicked the other Uhuru man out of. Harry grabbed Mohamid by the collar and threw him out the portal. A second later, the garage blew up.

The blast sent Harry smashing onto the attic stairs as

debris hurled in from the window. Glass shards and wood slivers splashed onto his back as he lay dazed. The explosion only served to fan the flames higher. When Harry's mind cleared, his shoe was smoldering.

He stamped out the small flame with his other shoe and retreated quickly up the steps, the fire covering the broken window. He kept low to the ground, but he couldn't keep from hacking because of the noxious cloud. He crawled into the right-hand room. Still lying stomach down, he shot out the small stained-glass window. He dragged himself over and looked out. It was a sixty-foot drop, straight down.

Harry rolled over onto his back and looked out the open door. A sheet of flame had leaped up between the two rooms. He took a deep breath, got up, ran over, and shot away both door jams. The door fell on his foot. His teeth gritted, his head pounding, and his lungs entirely closed off, Harry shoved his gun back, grabbed the door on both sides and charged out of the room.

He felt all the hair on his hands crisp up and blow away. An astonishing pain ripped through each finger and clamped onto his brain. He heard a horrible scream, but he couldn't tell if it was him or the devastating fire. He closed his eyes and ran until the door became too heavy and his legs wouldn't move anymore.

He fell forward into the other room. The door landed on its bottom corner and leaped against the wall. Harry's knees gave way and he slammed into the hot wood floor on his face. The first thing he saw when he came to seven seconds later were the backs of his hands stretched out in front of him. They looked like two teriyaki steaks well done. He was almost sorry he woke up. The pain and the heat started again.

Both were so intense, he couldn't help writhing on the floor. His mind went on automatic and screamed for the Magnum, but his charred hands couldn't grip it. His body took over. He rolled to the last window, brought his feet up and kicked the window out.

From that position, Harry could see the flames licking into the room behind him. The fire moved like waves—getting closer and closer every time. He didn't hesitate to check the drop. With a final effort, he reached up, grabbed the sides of the broken window and propelled himself out feet first.

The flames seemed to roar out of the window in anger after him as he plummeted sixteen feet to a side incline. He slammed against that, rolled down, hit another inclined roof right below that, and fell into a pile of sand that had collected against the side of the house. Harry didn't know the extent of his injuries, but he did know he wasn't dead.

Hands plucked at him. They rolled him over. Harry saw figures in blue and yellow uniforms. The cavalry had arrived. He was carried out to the safety of some ambulances across the street. He felt tired. He didn't feel good. The last thing he saw that day was the face of Captain Avery looking down at him with concern.

Harry laughed himself into unconsciousness.

Chapter Five

"You're extraordinarily lucky, Inspector Callahan," said Dr. Steve Rogers.

"Yeah, I know," Harry said from the hospital bed. "Wounded on a weekend. Won't even miss a day's work."

"Jesus, Harry, you know what I mean," said the seasoned police medico. "I've taped up bullet grooves on your legs and stitched gashes in your head, but this was cutting it too close."

The cop sat up in the private room wearing only a pair of pajama bottoms. Aside from a variety of small bandages across his face and torso, the only thing that looked bad were his hands. They looked like an abortive audition for a Mummy movie.

"Just superficial, right?" Callahan inquired, holding them up. "Only melted off the top layer?"

"Right," Rogers replied, packing up his black bag. "They'll be stiff for a couple of days, but workable. I'll be back to take off the heavy bandages tonight."

"Good," said Harry. "Thanks, Steve."

"No sweat," the doctor winked. "We hill boys have to stick together."

Before he could open the door, it swung back to reveal Lieutenant Bressler and Captain Avery. The superior officer walked brusquely in. The lieutenant followed, holding a small vase of flowers uncomfortably.

"Good afternoon, Doctor," Avery boomed. "Everything check out all right, I trust?"

"As well as can be expected," Rogers solemnly replied. He brushed by the captain but gave Harry another wink as he breezed out the door.

Everyone waited until it closed behind him. Then Bressler moved nervously forward, holding out the plants.

"Uh, the wife thought you'd like this, Harry," Bressler mumbled.

Harry held up his bandaged hands in a suppliant gesture.

"Oh, yeah, right," said the lieutenant, putting the vase on a side table. "Sorry."

"Tell her they're very nice," Harry said.

"Sure," Bressler agreed with relief.

"So, Harry," Avery blustered. "How do you feel?"

"How do you think I feel?"

"Sure, sure, I can understand that," the captain rolled right on. "I want to commend you on the first-class job you did in there, Inspector. I wouldn't be surprised if there was a special commendation for your bravery above and beyond the call of duty."

Harry folded his legs, laid his hands on his stomach, and smiled. "And I just want to say what a first-class idiot you are, Captain," he said pleasantly. "If it wasn't for your stupidity, I wouldn't have had to do anything above and beyond the call of duty."

A stillness close to death entered the hospital room. Bressler looked from Harry's smiling face to Avery's shocked one. He did that twice before trying to break the stalemate.

"Uh, Harry, aren't you being a little harsh. . . ?"

Harry held up his hands. Bressler fell silent.

"Just what are you trying to prove, Inspector?" the captain choked out, his face crimson.

"Nothing," Harry curtly replied. "I just wanted to get that off my chest."

The captain hastily pulled himself together. He straightened his uniform, cleared his throat, and looked sympathetically at Bressler. "Of course he's upset," he said, "who wouldn't be?" He looked expressionlessly at Harry. "We'll talk again. When you're feeling better." He had almost made it to the door when Harry spoke again.

"Just be glad I'm not trying to prove anything when the Internal boys come around."

Avery stopped cold with one hand on the door latch. He turned around. "Internal Affairs?" he said as if mentioning the Spanish Inquisition. "Have they been here?"

"Not yet," said Harry. "I just thought it would be nice to chat before they do."

"Chat?" echoed Avery, nervously coming over to the chair next to the bed. "What about?"

"About the deaths of . . . how many Uhurus? Six?"

"They were . . . are a militant group. They attacked a white girl. They, uh, even fired on you!"

"It doesn't hold together, Captain," Harry calmly explained. "You moved before the Steinbrunner autopsy report came in. I know. I had the report sent to my office as soon as it was finished. There was salt water in her lungs. Where was she going to get salt water in the Uhuru cellar?"

"They could've kidnapped her from the beach," Bressler suggested.

"The coroner figured she died at least twelve hours before we found her. What would she be doing on the beach in the middle of the night?"

"But the attack on you at the college and at the house . . . ," Avery reminded the inspector.

"Yeah," Harry drawled. "The three dudes came into the school with fucking assault rifles. New ones. The men at the Uhuru house had discontinued jobbies. Army-surplus junk. It doesn't make any sense."

"What do you want?" Avery demanded.

"I want a free hand," Callahan replied immediately. "I don't want your office and the D.A. hovering around

Mohamid's hospital bed like vultures, waiting for him to die so you can slap a warrant on his corpse."

"He's in a bad way, Harry," Bressler told him. "The gas cans exploding in the garage threw him away from the worst of it, but he still has a concussion and internal injuries from landing on the sidewalk."

"If he's awake, he'll help," Harry assured them.

"Just one thing, Inspector," Avery said brusquely, regaining some of his pomposity. "Why did Mohamid board his place up and open fire? What was the purpose of that?"

"He thought he was being railroaded again," Harry said simply. "When that first reporter confronted him about the letter, he said 'it's starting again.' The press had a field day with that, but what he meant was they were being framed again. The three blacks attacking me at Berkley was another bad sign."

"That's what set him off?" Bressler asked incredulously.

"No, there was something else. When I was running through the house, I recognized everyone I saw from the afternoon we found Steinbrunner's body. But there was someone missing. A girl."

"Well, that makes sense," the captain claimed. "They wouldn't want her in the middle of the firefight."

"Maybe," Harry admitted, "but I took the liberty of calling in one of the uniformed men who was guarding the house before everything happened. He reported that the girl left the house two hours *before* the Berkeley attack. And she wasn't dressed for hiding out. She was decked out for going out."

"That's slim," Avery contended.

"Yeah," Harry drawled. "But at least I don't have to kill a half dozen men to make my point."

The captain stiffened. "All right, Inspector," he said officiously. "You've got your free hand. I trust you'll have nothing undue to say to the Internal department."

"About what?" Harry asked innocently.

The captain nodded, stood, and went to the door. Before he left, he turned for a last parting shot. "But you had better pray you hold a full house. Because if you blow this one, I'll be waiting for you back at headquarters."

After he left, Bressler let out a sigh of relief. "Too tough, Harry," he said. "Too tough. You must really like risking your neck."

Callahan shrugged. "I've handed my star in before. I can do it again. It always seems to come back."

"Yeah. Callahan's boomerang badge. Now what about this girl?"

Just as Bressler finished his sentence, the hospital door swung open and Sergeant Lynne McConnell strode in with Fatso Devlin close behind.

"What timing," remarked Harry. "Can I offer you a seat, Sergeant?" he asked, nonchalantly flipping back the covers on his bed.

"Ooh, a gentleman!" McConnell exclaimed earthily. To everyone's surprise, she called Harry's bluff by striding over and sitting on the edge of the bed.

Bressler looked from Fatso's grinning puss to McConnell's mockingly innocent gaze to Harry's noncommittal one. He had never seen police officers acting this weird.

"Uh, take it easy, Harry," the lieutenant said, edging his way toward the door. "See you tomorrow, OK?"

"OK," Harry answered, looking at McConnell's well-delineated form next to him. "Take it easy."

"You too." Bressler left shaking his head and wondering whatever became of San Fran's finest.

"Some people just can't accept change," Devlin smirked.

"Yeah," said Harry. "Like me. Get off the bed, Sergeant."

McConnell smiled glowingly at him, then primly rose to occupy the chair Avery had left vacant. "Why, Inspector," she admonished, "don't you trust the new breed of policewoman?"

"No," said Harry without a trace of emotion. "They get killed as easily as the new breed of policeman." That sobered things up in a hurry. Playtime was over. "How's the case coming?" Harry asked anyone who'd answer.

"Lousy," McConnell answered, eager to make up for her *faux pas*. "Cunningham and Ramierz are up and talking, but neither has ever seen The Professor personally. They've talked to him over the phone, but they can't even identify the voice."

"So there's still no positive identification on him? No accurate description?"

"Nothing. The children he used differ in their stories as well. It looks like he uses disguises. Why?"

Harry looked at her young, clear, open, vivacious face hard before answering. "Just curious," he finally related. "No reason."

They chatted about nothing for a few minutes before Fatso explained that they had just droppd by to see how he was and they had to get back to work. Harry said he was tired anyway. Devlin waved from the door. The sergeant suddenly leaned down and kissed Callahan lightly. Without another word, she swept out of the room. Harry looked questionably at Devlin. Fatso shrugged and followed her.

Harry slowly put his hands behind his head. He stared up at the ceiling and thought. Hard.

If Big Ed Mohamid wasn't dying, he sure felt like he was. He'd drift back and forth into consciousness on a constant cloud of pain. Every time he slept, he relived the fire and the explosion. He felt himself falling, then he heard the blast; he felt himself floating away in a ball of heat, then something hit him. Hard. After that he felt himself being pulled across broken glass. Finally he woke up and felt the pain. When he closed his eyes, it all started over again.

For what felt like the hundredth time he opened his eyes. He became aware of someone at the end of his bed. He tried to get up, he tried to shout, but the pain wouldn't let him.

"I don't believe it," said a familiar voice. "Someone as big and black and dumb as you can't die."

Mohamid smiled. "Harry," he breathed painfully.

Dirty Harry Callahan knelt by the side of the bed,

showing the Uhuru leader his face in the dim light from outside.

"Why don't you turn on the lights, man?" Mohamid grunted.

"Don't want to make you too easy a target," Harry expounded. "Why aren't you dead already? I've been waiting all night for someone to make a move."

Mohamid turned his head gradually to the side. He saw that Harry was dressed completely in black; long-sleeved T-shirt, slacks, slip-on shoes. He was even wearing thin black gloves. In his right hand he held the Magnum.

"They're not going to kill me, man," Mohamid chuckled deep in the back of his throat. "That would blow their game. Then the fuzz would know I was being rung."

"It's safer to let you talk?"

Mohamid closed his eyes and grimaced. "No one would believe me. Except maybe you."

Harry nodded. "I'm listening."

Mohamid swallowed and licked his lips. "They got Rose, man. They got Rose for insurance. Or maybe they liked the way she looked. I don't know. These fuckers don't care. They do anything they want. They've got the bread."

"Come on," Harry stressed. "Who are they, Mohamid?"

"Slavers, jack, modern-day white slavers." Mohamid closed his eyes and smiled in agony. "Still believe me, Callahan?"

"I'm not going anywhere," Harry said flatly.

"They came to me. Knew my history. Burn whitey. Anything for a buck. They wanted me to point girls out. Girls a little too in-de-pendent. Girls who dated blacks. White chicks mostly, but they hinted they'd look at anybody. They said they give me $25,000 a head. That's how they put it . . . a head."

"You refused?" Harry asked.

"What? You kidding?" Mohamid replied with painful indignation. "Twenty-five grand is twenty-five grand. I said I'd think about it. You see some of the chicks we got running around, man? Wigglin' their asses, doing anything they like? Little sluts running around. A different guy every night. They want to be whores. They're just askin' for it."

"Rose asking for it?" Harry reminded him quietly, then adding a sarcastic "man."

Mohamid swallowed. "I guess I waited too long," he decided. "When Rose didn't come back, I called the number they gave me. They said I should admit to killing the white chick."

"What's the phone number?" Harry demanded. Mohamid gave it to him. Harry rose and went to the door.

"You see?" The man's tortured voice came out of the darkness from the bed. "They don't have to kill me. The courts'll do the job for 'em. Nobody'll buy that story in a million years."

"Maybe," Harry said and left the room.

Walking down the plain, fluorescent-filled hallway toward the phones, Harry considered disbelieving the story. He had heard rumors of a flourishing white slavery trade and a top eschelon police cover-up of the situation, but it didn't seem likely, even to him. There couldn't be enough money, and there were too many risks in abducting women. But then he remembered the thousands of people who disappear every year. Out of those it was quite possible that close to a hundred were good-looking females. And he remembered the San Francisco of the early 1900s. History has proven that then white slavery was a prosperous trade.

Harry reached a pay phone in the hallway. He slipped a dime in the slot and punched out the number Mohamid gave him.

"I'm sorry," said a raspy voice in his ear, "the number you have reached is not in service at this time. Please check your directory and try your call again. This is a recording."

Rose Ray heard a recording too, but its subject matter was completely different.

"Big Ed Mohamid raped the girl Barbara Steinbrunner.

He raped you. He murdered the girl Barbara Steinbrunner. He threatened to kill you if you talked."

The same message repeated over and over again into her ear. After a while it seemed to go directly into her brain. As much as she shook her head, the message wouldn't stop. As much as she tried to reach her ears to stop it, she couldn't move. As much as she tried to stuff up her ears, they were already stuffed with the message. As much as she tried to scream, no noise would come out.

Rose Ray was in a cell. A black, tight-fitting hood had been stitched around her head. Not tied, but stitched. The only way to get the hood off was to cut the stitching wires that laced up at the back of her skull. Inside the hood were two speakers that fit over her ears, two pads that fit over her eyes, and a large rubber shaft that filled her mouth.

She lay spread-eagled in midair, halfway between the floor and the ceiling. She was held aloft by a dozen straps that stretched from the floor to her limbs, then up to the ceiling. There was a tight, thick strap around her ankles, her thighs, her waist, above and below her breasts, her arms, and her wrists.

The only other thing she wore was an arrangement of straps around her hips. These held in the dildo which was always on when someone was not around to play with her. Then the vibrator was pulled out, and she would be gently swung back and forth in the horrible darkness until her raper was satisfied.

Occasionally she would be sat down so she could go to the bathroom. At the same time she would be injected with enough nutriments to stay alive. But the hood would never come off. And the message never ended.

"Big Ed Mohamid raped the girl Barbara Steinbrunner. He raped you. He murdered the girl Barbara Steinbrunner. He threatened to kill you if you talked."

It was a beautiful Monday morning in San Francisco. On a morning like it, sunny, sixty-three degrees, it would be hard for most people to really believe such things as rape, murder, child prostitution, and white slavery existed.

It was hard for Harry Callahan to believe as well, but that was what kept getting him up every morning and into work. He wanted to make it impossible to believe. Unfortunately, doing that involved risks, and the reality of the world sometimes made it difficult for Harry to take all of them himself, much as he wanted to.

Harry's black-gloved fists hit the top of a plain gray desk on either side of a nameplate reading, "Sgt. McConnell."

"How would you like to go back to school, Sergeant?" he asked.

"Oh?" said the policewoman, looking up at Harry's bruised face. "Do you have something to teach me?"

"Sergeant," Harry sighed, coming around to sit heavily on the chair beside her writing table, "can't we have a conversation that doesn't include sexual allusions?"

McConnell leaned across her typewriter. "Inspector Callahan," she admonished, then changed her tact. "May I call you Harry?" He nodded. "Harry, Harry, Harry," she readmonished, "you've got to be crazy if you think I'm going to let a hunk like you slip through my fingers."

"On your own time," Harry suggested in a warning tone. "We've got a job to do."

McConnell stopped smiling and leaned back. "I do my job, Inspector," she said seriously. "You know that. I'm sure you asked around about me."

"Everyone spoke highly of you," Harry admitted. "But I don't see it. What are you doing on the police force?"

"My job!" McConnell exclaimed. "Hey, Inspector, you don't hold the monopoly on wanting to improve the world, you know. Other people have convictions and morality, too."

"That's not the point. . . ."

"Harry," the policewoman scolded. "I've been here five years. I've seen whores with their faces carved. I've seen children dying of old age. I've seen the most ridiculous, cruel, stupid men. . . ."

"And you're still here."

"Hey, just because people are in pain, do I have to

106

stop living?" McConnell demanded with a quiet passion. "Do I have to trudge through life like a walking wounded because someone else did something stupid or destructive? I can help them, but I'm not going to suffer for them."

Harry couldn't deny the validity of her convictions, but he had his own crosses to bear. He wasn't doing anyone else's suffering, he was constantly mourning his own losses. Besides, he wasn't worrying about her past record, he was worrying about what he was planning to get her into.

McConnell saw something in his expression. "Harry, I'm not saying don't worry about me, I'll be all right. Worry about me all you want. I'd appreciate it. Just say what you want to say and let's get going."

Harry said it and they got going. Within a half an hour they were headed for the University of California at Berkeley.

"The second summer semester is about to start," Harry told her. "I want you to enroll in a few film courses, fill out an application for fall acceptance into the university, look for an apartment, and do all those funny little things new students from out of state do."

"Only film courses?" she wondered.

"Yeah. A girl as attractive as you won't arouse any suspicion. Every pretty girl from the Midwest wants to be a movie star."

"Why, Harry," the sergeant smirked, "I didn't know you cared."

Harry smirked back. "Fill your schedule so you'll be around all day. Be sure to take at least one course taught by Roy Hinkle."

"You have anything on Hinkle?"

"Nothing substantial. Just a solid hunch. . . ." Harry let the sentence trail off.

"That he's The Professor?" McConnell finished for him.

"You're way ahead of me," Harry concurred.

"It makes a modicum of sense," she elaborated. "If Mohamid didn't call the killers out on you, then Hinkle is the only logical choice. As Sherlock Holmes said, 'once

107

you've eliminated the impossible, whatever's left, however improbable, has to be the truth.' "

"Or words to that effect," Harry said as he turned onto Telegraph Avenue.

"Or words to that effect," the girl agreed. "And given that he's a college teacher, it's not out of the realm of possibility that his code name became The Professor."

Harry marveled at her deductions as well as her vocabulary. "No wonder they made you a sergeant," he mused.

McConnell looked over and flashed him one of her disarming smiles. "Wanna arm wrestle?" she suggested gayly.

"Not today, dear," Harry answered wearily. "I've got a headache." The inspector pulled the car over at the corner of Bancroft Way. "Now watch your ass," Harry recommended seriously. "From now on you're Jo Frawley, a Midwest orphan who never accepts dates from the same man twice. Don't lay it on thick, but get the point across."

"Thank you very much," McConnell said in a bored tone. "Care to give me any hints on my makeup?"

"Just remember," Harry continued, undaunted, "if Hinkle is The Professor and is tied in with these slavers, they'll be fast, vicious, and professional. Don't take any chances. Stay in touch always."

McConnell put her hand on Harry's shoulder. "I appreciate your concern, but take it easy, Harry. There'll be undercover guardian angels from vice all over the place. And if that fails, I'll always have you." She leaned forward and kissed him. "Now get out of here before someone recognizes you," she cracked and hopped outside the car. She walked away with her suitcase without looking back.

Harry watched her walk away in the student disguise of tight jeans over boots and a fuzzy, clinging sweater. There's a new girl in town, Harry thought, and an angry depression fogged in his mind. He would have felt better if she *had* been a student from the Midwest or a secretary or a nurse. Anything but a cop. Well, Harry concluded, slamming the car into gear, better a cop than a victim. And definitely not both.

He drove back to headquarters thinking about Inspector Kate Moore. She had been his sixth partner and the third to die. She was shot by a terrorist on Alcatraz Island. Harry had paid back her killer in kind for all the good it did her. He'd think about her from time to time. Not as often as he thought about his wife, but enough.

His wife had long before stopped being a person. She had become a deity that Harry remembered with a fondness he knew he wouldn't feel again. Kate was still a tangible being, a hardened innocent who tried so hard to be one of the boys. Lynne McConnell couldn't care less about that. She was a woman and proud of it. She didn't try to fit in, she just was.

That kind of mental security, that kind of psychological peace could prove very attractive. It could also prove infuriating. It could incite respect or it could incite a vengeful rage. It could lead to love or rape. The sad thing was that there was nothing anyone could really do about that. All one could do was live and hope that she was never at the wrong place at the wrong time.

Harry got back to headquarters to find out that Captain Avery was indeed waiting for him.

The captain, Lieutenant Bressler, and Fatso Devlin were all waiting for him in his office. A video-tape deck and television set on a cart had been wheeled and plugged in.

"Well, if it isn't the know-it-all inspector!" Avery announced loud enough for the whole floor to hear as Harry came in. "You have any more answers for us, Inspector?"

Callahan looked from Avery's flushed, exalted face to Bressler and Devlin who had taken up positions on the other side of the desk. Their lips were clamped shut. Harry wouldn't have been surprised if Avery had stapled them closed.

Rather than answering, Harry shook his head. It wasn't enough for Avery.

"No answers?" he demanded with vicious glee. "You mean you have absolutely nothing to say about the press conference?"

"What press conference?" Harry asked, knowing that it was exactly what Avery wanted him to say.

"What press conference?" Avery repeated in mock shock. "But I thought you had all the answers, Inspector Callahan. I thought you knew exactly what you were doing. If I had any idea you were in any way unsure I never would have assigned you the Steinbrunner case!" By the time he had finished the speech, the captain was shouting. He wanted to make sure everyone heard him disciplining his errant inspector.

No sooner had he collected more wind than he was expelling it again. "Well, for your information, Inspector, we found the missing Uhuru girl today. Do you happen to know what she said?"

Harry was damned if he did and damned if he didn't, so he decided to "did." "I already said no once," he said directly in Avery's face.

The captain's left eye almost closed completely as he glared back at Callahan. "Another answer," he marveled. "Well, it just so happens that I have a video tape of her meeting with reporters this morning. Would you care to take a few seconds out of your busy schedule to see it?"

Harry nodded curtly. Avery couldn't think of anything to say to that so he motioned for Bressler to turn the machine on.

A pale, nervous Negro girl in a red wraparound dress appeared on the screen, surrounded by a pushing lake of microphones, lights, and cameras. All manner of questions were being thrown at her as she tried to speak. She looked hysterically around until a gentle-looking man with high cheekbones and brown hair, pushed all the newsmen aside and put his arm around the obviously upset girl.

"One at a time please, one at a time," the man stressed. "Ms. Ray has had a terrifying experience. If you'll all just be patient, she will make a statement."

"Who's that?" Harry asked.

"Don't you know?" Avery inquired sarcastically.

"Her lawyer," said Devlin. The captain looked at Harry's partner with demotion in his eyes. Fatso grimaced and shut up.

The reporters had quieted in the meantime. Rose looked with trepidation from her lawyer to the line of microphones.

"Go ahead," said the lawyer.

"Big Ed Mohamid raped the girl Barbara Steinbrunner," she said in a tiny, thin voice. "He raped me. He murdered the Steinbrunner girl and threatened to murder me if I talked."

Immediately the flood of questions started again as the reporters moved back in. The lawyer tried to fend them off, but it was no good. Harry heard the black girl moaning, "he raped me," as the lawyer jostled her toward the car. The last shot in the report was a view along the side of the car taken from the front fender. As the lawyer pushed her head down so she could get into the car, Harry saw her face covered with tears.

"All right, all right," the lawyer yelled, getting in the car himself. "Ms. Ray has been through a horrible ordeal. She is still living in fear of her life. No more questions please."

And on that note, the limo door closed, and the lawyer, Rose Ray, as well as anyone else who had been inside, drove away.

Avery slammed the machine off. "Well, I hope you're satisfied, Inspector," he raged as Harry moved slowly behind his desk, deep in thought. "Mohamid was guilty all along, just as I said." Harry sat down, found a piece of paper and a pencil and started to work.

"Big Ed is still wounded and under police guard," Harry said quietly. "You can arrest him any time."

"I don't need your permission for that," the captain said, misunderstanding. "And from now on, Callahan, you report to me personally before you even go to the bathroom, is that clear?"

Harry looked up for a second, then returned his attention to the paper in front of him. He realized that Captain Avery had come down from his mountain because he thought he was safe. If Uhuru was guilty, then he had nothing to fear from Internal Affairs. So he wanted to secure his superiority with the rest of the men by dressing Harry down personally and in public.

Harry was in a very delicate situation. If he told Avery what he thought of him, the captain had plenty of witnesses when he brought Callahan up on charges. It was a perfect way of demoting him. But if he kissed ass, he'd lose a lot of self-respect. Normally, he wouldn't give a shit about insubordination or demotion, but another life was at stake. He had to stay on the case because of McConnell.

"Inspector Callahan," Avery roared. "Do we understand each other?"

Harry held up the piece of paper. On it was a readily identifiable drawing of a hand with every finger missing except the upraised middle one. "Yes sir," he said, and before anything could be done about it, he drew the forefinger in. "Perfectly."

Avery looked like his head would come completely off and go swooshing around the room. Harry kept his face expressionless. The captain clenched his fists, ground his upper teeth on his lower lip, and stalked out of the office.

"Christ, Harry," Bressler breathed. "What was on the paper?"

"A token of my esteem," the inspector replied.

"God, Harry," piped in Devlin. "I thought you were going to be thrown out of the game for sure."

"Yeah," Harry mused. "So did I. Why wasn't I, Al?"

"Come on into the office," Bressler said instead of answering Harry's question. "I don't know about you, but I need a drink."

Once everyone was inside Bressler's domain and the door was closed, the lieutenant got down to brass tacks.

"To tell you the truth, Harry," he started, "we didn't find the Rose girl. She just sorta appeared. We get a call from the networks, we turn on the set, and there she was."

"From what I can tell," Devlin interjected, "she was talking on the court steps."

"The TV people verify that," Bressler continued. "She comes down the steps, gives her statement, and gets in the car and just disappears. We go over to the courthouse to check it out, and not one lawyer or judge in the place has talked to the girl."

"What was her lawyer's name?" Callahan asked.

"He didn't give a name," Devlin answered. "He just said he was her lawyer."

"So it was just a 'media event,'" Harry theorized. "A media event that's just buried Mohamid."

"Looks that way," Bressler admitted. "Avery's out for his blood and it'll be hard to control the public now."

"Any chance of riot?" Harry inquired.

"If the Uhuru massacre didn't set it off, I don't think this will. After all, it was a sister telling on a brother. Not like some white cop shooting him in the back. We expect some peaceful demonstrations, but that's about all."

"Maybe Bob Dylan will write a song about him," Devlin suggested.

"Hope it'll do Big Ed more good than it did Hurricane Carter," Harry answered back. "You got an extra tape of the Rose news conference?" he asked Bressler.

"Yeah," the lieutenant said, reaching into his bottom drawer. "What do you want it for?"

"I'd like to get Mohamid's reaction. Maybe he's seen the lawyer around somewhere."

Bressler handed the tape cassette over the desk. Harry took it and got up to leave.

"Hey, listen, Harry," Bressler called to him. He turned back from the door. "Mohamid's no longer at the hospital."

"What?" Harry exploded.

"The captain moved him to a maximum-security police Surgery area right after the news conference this morning."

Harry was out of the office and running toward the elevators before Bressler even stopped speaking. Devlin raced out of the lieutenant's room in hot pursuit. The fat Irishman caught his partner between the elevators and the stairs.

"What's the matter?" he huffed.

"After the girl accused him, there's no more reason to keep him alive," Harry yelled, brushing by Fatso toward the emergency exit.

"You're not making any sense," Devlin called after him.

"Just get some men down to the cellar to back me up!" Harry shouted back, already flying down the steps. A jumbled set of points came together in his head as he hurtled down toward the basement. The slavers had completed their frame of Mohamid. They didn't need the black man to cry innocent on deaf ears anymore. In fact, it would be better if he wasn't around to defend himself at all. That way the package would be complete, and there'd be no one to question it or raise a fuss. Basically, they needed Ed to commit suicide.

In the hospital, it would have been hard. Any policeman worth his salt would have questioned a doctor he hadn't seen before. But what cop is going to question an orderly in the police station? Harry slammed open the emergency door on the bottom floor, The emergency alarm automatically went off. The cop kept going, ignoring the quizzical faces that appeared in the doorways he passed. Instead he barreled into the coroner's office and grabbed the first arm he could find. It happened to belong to an Oriental girl.

Harry pulled her away from her microscope and pushed his badge in front of her face. "Callahan," he said, "from upstairs. How long have you worked here?"

"Ahob, ahob, two years," the shocked girl replied.

"Come on then," Harry said, pulling her out of the room and down the hall. He saw Steve Rogers walking toward him. The doctor smiled and opened his mouth to greet his friend.

"Where's Mohamid?" Harry barked.

Rogers blinked in surprise, snapped his mouth shut, and pointed the way he had come. "Room B-14," he answered.

Harry went right by him without slowing, holding the

girl's hand. She had to run to keep up with his fast walk. "Thanks," he told the doctor in passing.

Harry turned the corner along the B-14 hall just as a stocky bald man walked out of one of the rooms. "Do you know him?" Callahan asked the girl.

"N-not really," the girl said with doubt.

"Have you seen him around at all?"

"No, I don't think so."

Harry spied B-17 to his right. It wasn't the room the bald man had left. "Quick," he instructed the girl, "go in B-17 and tell me who's there."

The Oriental, happy to get out of Harry's clutches, hurried over and pushed open the door. "Nobody," she said, not understanding a thing.

"Get inside and stay down!" he yelled at her before he bellowed after the bald man. "Hold it!"

The bald man didn't even turn around. Without flinching, he simply jumped through the door of the room at the end of the hall. Harry raced to the room that the man had last left.

He slammed against it with his shoulder. It was locked. He shot away the lock and kicked it open. Big Ed Mohamid hung from an overhead pipe by a police belt notched around his neck.

Harry brought his Magnum up and blasted. The bullet went right through the center of the leather belt, sending pieces in every direction and sending Mohamid to the floor. Harry didn't have time to check his condition. He ran from the room to the last door on the right. On the front were the neatly stenciled letters, "A-U-T-O-P-S-Y."

"Oh Christ," Harry breathed as Fatso rounded the corner with four other men. "Stay there," Harry called to him. "There's a maniac in here I want to talk to."

The inspector pushed open the barrier and dove in. The slick floor was perfect for sliding. Harry skimmed almost all the way to the side wall. He stopped right behind a locker as a bullet whined off its metal front.

Harry checked his position. He was on the right side of a long room lined with lockers and dotted with tables. On the tables were bodies. They were blue and looked cold.

115

From where he was standing, he could see a completely naked old woman and a middle-aged man. Pulling his gaze away from the motionless corpses, Harry concentrated on not becoming one of them.

"Come on," he called. "There's no other way out. You know you don't stand a chance." Harry waited, but there was no answer. The bald man didn't want to give away his position by shouting back, and he didn't want to waste his ammo by shooting again.

Well, Harry figured, if you want anything done, you've got to do it yourself. The cop jumped from his locker cover to behind the table with the dead old woman on it. The dead old woman's stomach ripped open and a fountain of blood and other liquid gouted up. Harry heard the gun report right afterward. He fired back in the general direction as the woman's fluid flecked the side of his face. He heard the smashing of glass in front of him.

Callahan dodged behind the middle-aged man's table. Another bullet tore up some tile by his right foot. Harry dropped to his knees, seeing the bald man between the legs of a table all the way down the room. His adversary threw himself flat as Harry blasted away. The cop heard a satisfying yell of pain as one of his slugs gouged across the bald man's upright back. His other bullets tore away at the underside of the table and one of its legs.

Harry stood as the bald man pulled himself upright. The villain staggered back and crashed against some more lockers. He used them for leverage as he tried to get a bead on Harry. Callahan zigzagged toward him, keeping behind another set of tables. In panic, the bald man fired twice more, tearing off the top of a hippie corpse's head and punching a third nostril in the young man's nose.

Harry directed himself to the right, but the hippie's guts got in the way. He felt his shoe connect with something slick, and he fell. The bald man took advantage of the situation by running between tables and aiming at Harry's prone chest. Callahan grabbed the table and pulled it over just as the bald man fired.

Flesh and wood fell into the path of the bald man's bullet. The lead tore through the hippie's ribs and dug its way into the wood. It cracked through and sped over

Harry's chest and under his arm to clatter on the tile. The corpse flopped down on its side, a large crack echoing through the room, as Harry hurled the table out of his way with a powerful kick. He pulled himself to his feet to confront the bald man.

The bald man stared angrily at the rising cop. He held his weapon on a level with Harry's chest. Callahan recognized the gun. It was a 380 ACP-caliber F.I. Model D manufactured in America by Astra. It carried six rounds in the clip and one in the chamber. The bald man was out of ammunition. Harry, on the other hand, had two bullets left. He brought his Magnum up to the same level as the other man's Astra.

Facing the cop's big gun, the bald man seemed to panic. He backed away slowly, his tense face showing signs of fear. Harry moved forward, pacing him, holding the .44 steady and straight. The man passed between the last two tables. Out of the corner of his eyes, Harry saw two black men on the tops. The bald man kept moving back. He veered off to Harry's right, his gun hand getting shaky.

Finally there was no more room to move. The bald man had backed into a corner. He lifted his gun up toward Harry's face. Harry lifted his toward his opponent. They looked down each other's barrels. Two seconds passed and the bald man let his Astra droop. He lowered his head and pulled the gun's trigger. The room echoed with an empty click. Harry smiled.

Then the black corpse behind him sat up.

If Harry had seen it, his first thought would be muscle spasm. He had seen dead bodies in the morgue bend their arms and legs from involuntary muscle spasms. But he didn't see the black man rise behind him. And he didn't see him open his eyes. Harry only felt the black man's big fists smash into his kidneys.

The cop stumbled forward, the Magnum erupting harmlessly to the left. The bald man reared up and slugged the off-balance inspector in the face. Harry's head snapped back into the black man's grip. Two muscular arms wrapped around his head and neck in a hammerlock. The bald man grabbed his gun wrist in both hands.

117

Harry felt the black man's nudity against his back. He felt the thick limbs crushing down on his windpipe and pushing against the back of his head. He tried to pull the Magnum back, but the bald man held it forward. The trio staggered around the back of the autopsy room in a struggling clump.

One of the black man's hands grabbed a fistfull of Harry's hair. The bald man let go with his right and started pummeling Callahan in the stomach. Harry knew what they were planning to do. Once he had weakened sufficiently, the black man would snap his head to the side and hopefully break his neck. As the rumbling pain from his stomach and the lack of air reached his brain, Harry had to admit it was possible.

He went limp. His weight pulled the black man forward and made the bald man step back. Then Harry put all his muscles into overdrive. He pulled his gun arm back while throwing the other hand forward. The bottom of his palm slammed in the bald man's nose. A circle of blood splattered out onto his face. He swung the gun back into the black man's head. He heard a meaty thunk, and the grip relaxed around his neck.

Harry himself spun about, having to fall halfway across the empty autopsy table to catch his breath. He heard a noise behind and to his right. He swung the Magnum around as hard as he could. It slammed into the black's forehead. The man fell flat on his back.

Harry pivoted toward the bald man. He was on his knees, jamming some new shells into his weapon's magazine as blood continued to stream out of his nose. As soon as he realized that Harry was turning toward him, he tried pushing the clip back into the gun and firing it at the same time. But before the magazine had even clipped into place, Harry fired his last bullet point blank into the bald man's hand.

The man's hand was hurled backward, entire fingers literally being blown off. Two columns of blood foamed out of the hand like a bottle of champagne that had just been opened. The bald man fell on his destroyed nose, his ruined hand outstretched. The black man began to come to, his eyes blinking and his head shaking. Harry heard the door open behind him.

He whirled to see Fatso Devlin at the other end of the room. "Get out of here!" Harry shouted. His partner simply closed the door and told the other cops that it was a false alarm. Nothing to worry about. Then he stood against the autopsy room door from the outside, looking nonchalantly at his fingernails.

Inside Harry went over to the groggy nude black man, put a hand on his nodding forehead and hammered his head on the floor. Then he ran over to the writhing bald man, who was pushing his mangled hand into his other, trying to stem the flow of blood. He looked up as Harry approached. Harry kicked him in the jaw. The bald man flew back, his hands flung behind him.

He landed spread-eagled on his back, the torrent of blood from his shot-off fingers having left a double-banded trail of his fall. Harry dodged the slopping liquid as it splashed on the tile, then leaned down to rip off a strip from the bald man's lab coat. He tore it from the hem to the man's arm, then ripped it off sideways. He quickly tied a tourniquet around the man's upper arm. The blood flow diminished, then slowed to a thin stream.

Harry reached back and took out a pair of handcuffs from under his belt. He cuffed the bald man's good left hand to his left ankle. He then started going through the lockers. He pulled out two lab coats and a syringe. Harry laid those on the empty table and went to the coroner's desk. He pulled the reading lamp out of its socket and tore the wire out the back. He went through the drawers and found an extension cord. With these in hand, he approached the unconscious black man.

The naked man was awakened by some sharp slaps on his face. He looked up to see Harry's smiling face framed by an operating lamp. He tried to smash the face, but his arms and legs were twisted back behind him. He looked at himself. He was lying on the table he had been on before, only this time his arms were bent back over his head and over the edge of the table. They were tied by wire and lab-coat cloth, which stretched under the table

119

to his ankles, which were tied similarly. The cording was tight, keeping his big black body taut across the slab top.

The black man looked around. Behind Harry he saw the bald man half hog-tied by the one pair of handcuffs. Blood still leaked from his stumpy palm.

"Just a minute," said Harry, picking up the syringe, which was filled with a clear liquid. Harry walked over, reached down and roughly pulled the bald man's pants down, exposing his ass. Harry injected the fluid just above his right cheek. "That ought to do it," Harry remarked, returning to the table.

"Hey, man, what the fuck do you think you're doing?" the black man boomed. "You can't do this, man."

"Uh-huh," Harry agreed, plugging something into the handy socket on the leg of the table. "You know," he commented, "it may not look like it, but this room is really very well designed." Harry pointed up. "It has water jets in the ceiling." Harry pointed down. "It has gratings in the floor. I bet you could kill a herd of elephants in here and still have the place spotless in an hour. What do you say?"

"You're crazy!" the black man shouted.

"Wrong answer," Harry quietly told him. He raised his right hand. In it was a miniature buzz saw, the kind of hand held scalpel medical examiners use to make dissecting easier. There was a button on the side of the thick tube. Harry pressed it. The thin, sharp blade spun around with a grating, whirring sound. The black man's eyes bulged.

"What are you going to do with that?" he asked, his voice quaking.

"Punctuate our conversation," Harry said. "You say something right, and there'll be a period. You say something I don't like and I'll draw exclamation points all over your body."

The black man stared at Harry's placid face and the electric scalpel. Then he started to laugh. He roared with delight, his head going back between his bound hands.

"Naw, you ain't gonna do shit with that thing, man," he told Harry with assurance. "This is police headquarters. You touch me and all bets are off. I'll never even get to court. You'll lose your job. Forget it man, you're bluffing."

Harry stood stock-still for a moment. The black man was sure he was going to lean over and untie him. Instead Harry turned the saw on and sliced a cut along the black man's thigh.

The man screamed in surprise, his body bucking against the wire and cloth cords. Harry brought the still-whirring blade next to his face. The black man became very still and very quiet very quickly.

"I'm not going to bring you to court," Harry informed him. "I'm going to send you to hell. You're a corpse, remember? You were lying on a slab when I came in. Now all I have to do is find your clothes bunched in one of these lockers and burn them so no one will know the difference. What's another dead person here or there?"

"Christ, man," the tied man cried. "You cut me."

"The coroner cut you when he started your autopsy," Harry corrected him.

"Nobody'll buy it," the black yelled as a last ditch argument. "Tony'll tell them I was with him!" The black man motioned his head toward the unconscious bald man.

"Tony'll be out for a long time," Harry assured him. "Maybe forever. And if he wakes up, who'll believe him? And even if they do, you won't be around to see it." Harry started up the machine and sliced his other leg along the calf.

The black man screamed again, pulling himself left and right in an effort to escape. His heart pounded, creating two red waterfalls down his leg.

"Scream all you want," Harry said calmly. "The room is soundproof."

"What do you want?" the man howled, sweat pouring across his body. "Man, you're killing me!"

"Like you killed Barbara Steinbrunner?"

"Man, I swear I had nothin' to do with that! On my mother's grave!"

"Don't bring your mother into this. You'll be with her soon enough."

"Christ! I swear! I swear!" the black man babbled. "It was Tony. Tony did it to her!"

"What about the others?" Harry asked, holding the scalpel over the black man's head.

"What others?" he asked immediately.

Harry turned the device on. The black began screaming and writhing again. Harry slapped his free hand on the man's right hip. He brought the sharp, whirring blade close to the man's penis.

"Please!" the man shrieked. "Please, oh God, no! All right, all right, I'll tell you everything you want to know! Please don't!"

Harry kept the blade a centimeter from the organ, looking back up at the black man's face. "Go on," he instructed.

"I pointed some chicks out," the black man gibbered. "Whores, runaways, shit like that. They called me. Had me sit in a Caddy with another girl. That's all! I swear, that's all!"

"What girl?"

"I don't know, man," said the black, getting bolder. "Some black chick all dressed up."

"Red dress?"

"No, man, dressed like a boy! All these straps and makeup."

Harry cut away the very surface of the man's penis. The black man shrieked in agony, straining at his bonds. He had pulled so hard at the cords that his wrists were beginning to bleed almost as bad as his legs.

"I swear that's the truth!" he hollered up at the ceiling.

"Where did you take her?"

"Some disco, man. A disco in Emeryville. Off the bridge."

"I know where Emeryville is," Harry said warningly.

"It's right near the bay," the man hastily added. "Right at the end of a marsh. Near Route 15. Madame's, it's called. Madame's!"

"Thank you," snapped Harry, bringing the electric scalpel up, then down toward the man's throat. The black stiffened, gritted his teeth, and screwed his eyes shut.

Harry just kept bringing the saw down until it cut away the wire binding the black's wrists to his ankles. The man opened his eyes in astonishment. "Get dressed," Harry advised him, cutting away the rest of the bondage.

Harry pulled the plug out and brought the scalpel back to the coroner's desk. The man watched until the cop had turned back to him and pulled out his Magnum. The black hastened to a locker near the table and pulled out his clothes. Callahan waited until the man's pants were painfully drawn on over his bleeding legs and crotch. He then took him by the arm and led him toward the door.

Harry pulled the door open, nearly dropping Fatso Devlin on his back. The Irish cop stumbled backward, his arms windmilling to keep his balance. When he had regained his equilibrium, Harry hooked a thumb toward the back of the room.

"A little package for Captain Avery," Harry said, "telling him how much I appreciated his moving Mohamid."

"Big Ed is beyond caring," Fatso informed him.

Harry didn't say anything. The black man took it as a silent indictment.

"I didn't do it," he swore. "I was just look out for Tony."

"Shut up," Harry snapped. Devlin glanced questionably at the black man wearing just his pants. "You didn't see him," Harry demanded of his partner.

"Right," Devlin agreed, walking back toward the bleeding Tony.

Harry hauled the black around the corner and down the hall to the basement exit. He pushed the door open, and they walked outside. "Where's your car?" Harry asked his prisoner.

"Down the alley," the man motioned behind them. The pair hustled down the way until they came to a dark blue Oldsmobile.

"The keys," Harry demanded, putting his hand out.

The black man reached painfully into his pocket and brought out a key chain with three keys on one end and the astrological sign of Pisces on the other. Harry took the whole thing and unlocked the passenger door. "All right, Fish," Harry said, coining a nickname for him from the horoscope figure. "Get lost."

"Say what?" said the surprised Fish.

"You heard me," Harry said threateningly. "Get out of town, get out of state, get off the planet if you think that'll get you far enough away from me. Because if I ever see you again, I *will* kill you. And believe me, it'll hurt a lot worse and take a lot longer than what I did in there."

The look on Callahan's face stopped whatever doubting words the black man might have uttered. Without a sound, he scrambled across the car's front seat. Harry threw the keys after him. Within ten seconds the auto with the black man was speeding down the street.

Harry watched him go. You were right, he was thinking. There would have been no way to get him into court without self-destructing his police career. Cops all over the country were learning the same lesson in less extreme circumstances. It was easier and cheaper to administer backstreet justice than haul every asshole up on charges. The police do one thing wrong, and they find themselves hung on a lawsuit.

Harry probably could've been sued, but he would have been up on departmental charges for sure if someone like Avery knew what he had done. Thankfully, with a partner like Devlin, there was little chance of it. Harry wouldn't have been surprised if Fatso had already cleaned up the blood stains left by the black's wounds on the hallway floor.

Callahan got back inside just as Big Ed Mohamid's body was being carried down the hall to the morgue. Devlin wandered over to stand by Harry in the brightly lit cellar passage.

"I guess we'll never know whether he was guilty or not," Fatso said about the late black leader.

Harry considered telling Devlin everything. Just as quickly he decided not to. Harry had learned the hard way not to divulge dangerous information unless the listener was directly threatened by the danger. He had lost his fourth partner that way. Inspector Early Smith had been blown to kingdom come by a mailbox bomb after

Harry filled him in on a vigilante force inside the police department.

"I guess not," he said to Devlin.

The black man Harry had called Fish tore around his North Beach apartment, hurling things into an open suitcase on his living room floor. He wanted to take along only his necessities, but he couldn't find them. The checkbook, the bank book, and his clothes were all there, but he couldn't find his .32. The snubnose he usually kept behind the refrigerator was gone. The black man had stopped to think where he might have put it when the bathroom door opened.

Two of his brothers, who both had been in the Cadillac that night, burst out from the doorway and grabbed the black man by the sink. The gentle white man with the hair and cheekbones followed at a more leisurely pace.

The black brothers grabbed one arm each and pinned Fish to the front of his gas stove.

"Anthony did not report within his allotted time," the gentleman said quietly. "We began to worry."

The gentleman civilly reached down and turned on the gas for the burner directly below Fish's head. The black man smelled the fumes as they rolled across his face.

The captor to his right grabbed his hair and pushed his face inches from the burner. The gentleman, meanwhile, had pulled out a pipe from his jacket pocket. He slowly packed it and damped it down while Fish choked and coughed. Finally he pulled out a boxed kitchen match. He lit it as well as his pipe. But he did not shake it out. The message was clear.

"Give me a reason not to kill you," the gentleman requested.

Chapter Six

Lynne McConnell was feeling good about herself. The way she should, about herself. She had signed up for five courses, including Independent Filmmakers' Spectrum, went to five different apartment interviews, spent some time touring the campus, and just generally shook her bootie all over the place. It was what, in her experience, one might call a "Pepsi day."

It was a good beginning to what looked to be a long stake-out. Although she had played the vivacious country girl, outgoing and guileless, during continuous conversations with whoever was around, she figured it wouldn't be until she started taking the classes that Hinkle would notice her. But when he did, he only had to ask around or check her registration to get the fake story.

In the meantime, she had gotten a room at the Berkeley Inn Hotel until she heard from the landlords about the various available apartments. The handsome red brick building was a couple of blocks away from the campus. It was pretty drab but clean. It had telephones in the rooms but not a john. One had to go down the hall for that.

McConnell changed from her sweater and jeans to a slightly more revealing combination of a light plaid skirt and an elastic tube top with shoulder straps. She slipped on some medium-heeled cork sandals and prepared to go downstairs for dinner. She sat on the edge of the bed and wondered whether she should report in before or after she ate.

She looked around the room. No TV and hardly enough room to play solitaire. It was going to be a long night, she decided. She'd save her phone calls for later. She hopped off the sagging bed, pulled a light jacket out of her open suitcase on the chair, and left the room.

She passed an old washwoman halfway down the hall. The lady was toiling on the floor outside the ladies room. It made quite a picture. Lynne felt positively gothic in the declining hotel's graying hall way lit by fading yellow bulbs. The old woman toiling on her hands and knees completed the image. She was suddenly very eager to get out, but figured she'd better visit the bathroom.

"Excuse me," McConnell said to the maid as she skipped around her, pushed open the door, and entered the white tiled bath. She got a glimpse of streaked hair and looped earrings under the washwoman's kerchief before she took in the rustic charm of the washroom. It was fairly classic. Two sinks on the right wall. Two enclosed toilets on the left wall. An old, pull-down window on the far wall, complete with chain, and a table behind the entrance door, outfitted with special makeup mirrors.

McConnell went into the bathroom, washed her hands, and sat down in front of the mirror to touch up her face. There was not much to do. Her mascara and eye liner had made it through the day. Perhaps just a touch more highlight on her cheeks and some lip gloss. She set about her work, just as the door opened and the washwoman pulled her pail, brush, and mop in. Without turning around, she too set about her work.

McConnell smiled mirthlessly at the washwoman's back, comparing their respective duties. Well, she thought, turning back to the mirror, there, but for the grace of God, go I. As she touched up her cheeks, there was movement in the corner of her eye. Her peripheral vision picked it up, but McConnell didn't see the wash-woman lean down and pull a sponge out of a plastic bag next to her pail. She didn't really notice the washwoman mopping the front section of the floor so that she wound up directly behind her.

No, McConnell was too involved in making herself the most attractive target possible to feel the cross hairs on her. She stood up, pushing back the chair, and leaned over a few inches from the mirror to apply the lip gloss. She dipped the wand in the holder. She held the applicator up. And the washwoman pushed her forehead into the glass.

A sharp crack sounded in the washroom. A sharp crack broke across the mirror. A thunder clap and a lightning bolt of pain rifled into her brain. Her reflection disappeared under a heavy red curtain. She felt her legs give out. She felt her hands grab the edge of the makeup table. She tried to turn and fight.

The washwoman helped her. Suddenly tall and fast, the washwoman spun the groggy girl around, bent her backward over the table, jammed her knee up McConnell's skirt and between her legs until the policewoman's crotch stopped it, and clamped the sodden sponge over McConnell's mouth.

As the pain on her forehead diminished and her vision cleared, a different sensation took over. For a split second McConnell could see the washwoman's young face snarling with glee. She could see the washwoman's muscular arm vibrating with pressure. She could see the craggy, soft thing over her mouth and nose. She brought her fists up only to feel them stop and float in midair. The white tile all around her began to grow fuzz. The washwoman's face turned a deep orange then began to wash away.

She felt the small of her back against the edge of the table. She felt her feet slipping across the floor. She felt her arms drop. She smelled the sickly sweet aroma of the chloroform. The whole image of what was happening to her stopped and strobed. Then purple, exploding darkness.

The woman checked the outside hall. No one else was on the floor. She went to the door opposite the lavatory and knocked once. The gentleman flung it open. They both went back to the john, carried the girl to the room they had reserved that evening, and went to work on her.

Harry couldn't wait anymore. He had had a tough afternoon. Between filling out the forms on Tony's no-last-name arrest, checking with the vice squad to see if Lynne had reported, running to the hospital to see if the bald man had come out of his blood-loss coma, and filing to get a search warrant for Madame's, Harry was doing a lot but getting nothing done.

When McConnell hadn't reported in by five, Callahan figured he'd take a drive over to the campus on his own time. Maybe he'd drop by Emeryville on his way back for a quick drink. When the Emeryville exit came up on Route 80, however, Harry took it. He stopped by the nearest gas station, had the attendant fill the tank, and headed for the pay phone.

No, Harry thought. He couldn't risk blowing McConnell's cover no matter how much he'd like to see her. Dialing vice's number, Harry cursed himself. Her femininity was affecting his job. He had been seriously considering doing something he never would have considered doing to a fellow male officer. When was the last time he had risked blowing a guy's cover to join him for dinner?

Ron Caputo of Missing Persons answered. He had been on the case since Rose Ray had been officially reported missing.

"No, nothing yet, Harry," he said. "The vice boys say it isn't like her to wait this long."

"How about her guardian angel?" Callahan inquired. "He report in yet?"

"Yeah, at about 4:30," Caputo answered. "He said he was still waiting for her to contact him as to where she'd be staying the night."

"Where's he staying?"

"The Berkeley Youth Hostel on Harrison Street," the Missing Person's man replied. "He's going under the cover name of Mike Porter."

"Mike Porter. Got it," Harry said. "Thanks Ron." After he had hung up, Harry checked his watch. It was

:45. Depression gnawed at him again. The case was slipping out of his control. He paced back to his car, cursing McConnell this time. Trust a woman to be unprofessional, he caught himself thinking. Once he had gotten behind the wheel, however, he realized McConnell would never have allowed herself to be late unless there was a good reason. She may not want to be one of the boys, but she had too much pride in herself to be unprofessional. Something had to be going on. Or something had to be wrong.

Harry got back on Route 80 and sped up to Berkeley like he had his siren on. He made it to Harrison Street in record time. The deskman at the Youth Hostel was impressed by the rugged-looking man in the brown tweed jacket. Usually they only got pimply-faced, bearded transients in the five-dollar-a-night crash pad. He pointed the tall man back toward the rear of the first floor dormitory.

"Popular guy," the desk man commented as Harry moved away. "You're the second one who asked for him tonight."

Harry stopped in his tracks. "A woman?" he asked over his shoulder.

"Don't worry," the deskman assured him. "A man."

A chill swam across Harry's shoulders. "What did he look like?"

"Oh, medium height. Brown hair. Gorgeous facial structure."

"High cheekbones?" Harry pressed. "Did he look . . . gentle?"

"Positively angelic," the desk man concurred. Harry turned away, his expression as set and ashen as rock. "Now, now," the effeminate deskman called as Harry strode toward Porter's bed, "no jealousy!"

The hostel was set up the same as many bowery flophouses. There was simply a row of bunk beds against each wall with an aisle down the middle. The second floor was the same, only reserved for girls. The third floor had a couple of rooms reserved for couples. Harry walked to the very end of the aisle. He looked back at the front desk. The man there pointed to the left. Harry approached the sleeping structure. There was a young man

131

reading on the bottom bunk and another sleeping on the top.

"Mike?" Harry asked the reading one.

Without looking up, the reader motioned toward the top bunk with his thumb. Harry moved closer. The one on top was sleeping on his stomach with the pillow over his head.

"Mike?" Harry asked again. No answer.

Harry lifted the pillow. The undercover vice cop's head was turned in his direction. Porter's eyes were wide open and his mouth was scrunched against the mattress. He looked right through Harry. Callahan took hold of his arm and lifted. Sunday editions of both the Los Angeles *Times* and San Francisco *Examiner* were stuck between the corpse's chest and the bed. They were almost completely soaked through with blood.

Harry put the man back into place. He moved silently back to the aisle, then slowly at first but with increasing speed, walked out of the hostel.

"Have a nice night!" the deskman called after him.

Harry ran down the one block to Telegraph Avenue and the campus. He raced into the Student Union to find a map. A different girl was behind the Information desk but she told him how to get to the Registrar. Harry tried to figure out what happened on the way there.

Somehow the slavers had discovered Porter's presence on the scene. And if they had gotten to him, they must have known about McConnell as well. The only thing Harry couldn't fathom was how. It was impossible unless there was someone on the inside. Harry ran across the street, past the Golden Bear Restaurant. On the window was a sign that read, "Fresh Vegetables, Freshly Baked Desserts, Fresh Fish."

The face of a black man came into Harry's brain. He nearly stopped when the pieces fell together, but when he realized the meaning of the situation, he ran even faster. The Registrar's office was cooperative when they saw his badge. He just prayed that McConnell had put where she was staying on the college application. After too long a time to suit Callahan, a lady with lead-colored hair found o Frawley's sheet. Harry grabbed it out of her hand. He skimmed down the page until he saw "Berkeley Inn Hotel."

By the time he got back to his car, his chest felt like the inside of a Brillo pad. He pulled the door open, fell in, and pushed the key into the ignition. This trip he turned on his siren and stuck the flashing bulb up on the roof. He turned onto Haste Street seconds later, driving right up onto the hotel's lawn. He took in the street scene completely as he ran toward the lobby. Parked cars, a van, a carpet-cleaning truck, and a lot of motorcycles.

Harry stormed into the oak-paneled lobby with his gun out. He vaulted over two couches and grabbed the deskman by the collar.

"Lynne . . . I mean Jo Frawley," he shouted. "Police business!"

The desk man had lived through the student riots of the sixties. He took orders very well. He gave Harry a number on the third floor.

Harry took the steps two at a time, his legs beginning to feel like cooked macaroni. He went up to Lynne's door and kicked it open. The room was empty. He was about to spin around when he heard a loud engine roar into life below her window. Harry jumped over the bed and threw up the glass.

Below, on the street, he saw the carpet-cleaning truck rev its engine. In the back of the truck he saw two figures in overalls loading a large, rolled-up green carpet.

"Hold it!" Harry shouted out the window. "Freeze!"

The motor was too loud for him to be heard from so high up. He pointed his weapon out the window. He stopped just before he pulled the trigger. The carpet men didn't know he was there yet. If he fired, they'd either assume it was another vehicle backfiring or he'd give himself away prematurely.

Instead he turned and headed back down the stairs, grabbing the banisters in both hands and swinging down the flights one half at a time. He raced across the lobby shouting at the deskman as he went.

"Call the police! Carpet truck pointed north on

133

Haste!" Harry didn't care whether the hotel man responded or not. He'd take care of it as soon as he got into his car.

His adrenalin keeping his weary limbs pumping, Callahan dashed around the side of the building. The carpet truck was pulling out into the road. Instead of trying to catch up on foot, Harry sprinted to his vehicle on the lawn. He was in with the motor running before the truck had even gotten to the corner. Harry backed off the grass, ripping off huge divots as he went.

The truck rumbled slowly off to the north. Harry whirled his car to the east. He screamed around the corner parallel to the truck, almost wiping out three motorcyclists in the process. He wrenched the wheel to the side, narrowly missing the helmeted trio. Two screamed by him on one bike, the driver's girlfriend clutching him tightly around the waist. Harry saw his own reflection in the full head gear they wore. The second bike swerved onto the sidewalk to give Callahan's car plenty of room. The second driver shook a fist at him as he screeched down the remainder of the street.

He took his first left, his car veering all the way across the road. He pulled it back straight and located the rear of the carpet truck barreling down a hill a block away. Harry tore down the almost deserted college street, passing what cars there were with reckless abandon.

Harry went through the stop sign at the intersection where the carpet truck had turned left. Another car was trying to get through. Harry spun his wheel to the right, but it wasn't enough. He was slammed into the dashboard and his unmarked police car got a mark all the way down the side. The other car's headlights were smashed off and it spun sideways, blocking Haste Street. Harry jammed down the accelerator and kept going.

He catapulted off the top of the hill going sixty miles an hour in a twenty-five-mile-an-hour zone. All four wheels left the concrete for two seconds, then he crashed back down, his shocks singing with the pressure. The big police car waffled across the line, then straightened.

Harry saw the carpet truck at the bottom of the hill. It had slowed for a red light that was turning green. Its ight-hand blinker was on. Harry hauled out his .44 with is right hand, then slapped it into his left. He gripped the teering wheel with his knees and slapped his right hand n the horn. The car shrieked down the hill while Harry ook aim.

He was fifty feet away when he fired. The right rear re on the carpet truck blew just as it was taking the orner. Harry threw his gun to the seat and grabbed the heel with both hands. He turned the car right for the idewalk corner. Before the truck could accelerate even ith the flat, Harry's car had jumped the curb, smashed to a crowd of garbage cans and skidded broadside in ront of the six-wheeler.

Harry propelled himself out the open window, his Magnum in hand. The burly truck driver was getting out f the cab, his mouth on automatic, when he saw Harry's un. He threw himself back against the fender, his hands p. Harry grabbed him by the shoulder, whirled him round, and threw him toward the rear of the truck.

"Who's in there?" he shouted.

"Nobody, nobody!" the driver swore. "Just Bernie and es. I swear!"

"Call them out!" Harry demanded. The driver com-lied. The rear door swung open, the pair of movers ursing about the sudden stop.

"On your faces!" Harry shouted. "On the ground! ow!"

The three men dropped as if they had been decked by Mohammed Ali.

"Hands behind your head," Harry instructed. They omplied. "Don't move." The cop vaulted into the back f the truck, his gun at the ready. Inside there were steam quipment, vacuums, shampooers, vats of cleaning solu-on, and the green carpet.

It was big enough, Harry thought, looking at its rolled ngth. All they would have to do is knock McConnell ut, wrap her up in the rug, and carry her out. They'd ave to wait until the owner of the hotel had gone and the ight shift had come on. Then they could have told the esk anything.

Harry kneeled down at the end of the carpet and

looked down through the middle. Nothing was inside. No victim, no policewoman, no McConnell. The impact of the discovery was worse than looking down a hitman's gun barrel. The realization made him sick at heart.

It was all a coincidence. A miserable coincidence. Harry visualized the black man on the autopsy slab. He had said that they had disguised Rose Ray as a boy and tied her up. Any group that imaginatively perverted wouldn't have settled for anything as obvious as a carpet truck. Harry visualized the motorcyclists he had nearly run down. He remembered their helmets; all had black plastic visors that completely covered their faces.

He remembered the "girlfriend" of the first cyclist. How she clung tightly around his waist. He remembered the only part of her head he could see. Her hair. Her full lustrous brown hair flying in the wind.

Harry jumped off the back of the truck. "Get up," he told the lying men. They moved to their feet hesitantly. They all looked relieved as Harry put his gun away, and the sound of a siren came from down the street. The hotel man had called the cops after all.

"Tell them it was a misunderstanding," Harry said to the driver. "Tell them to call Dirty Harry for an explanation." Without waiting for a retort, Harry turned and walked through the gathering crowd of curious bystanders to his car.

"Hey!" the driver yelled after him. "Who's going to pay for my tire?"

"Who the hell do you think?" Harry spat. "Call the SFPD. Call Captain Avery. Tell him to put it on my tab." Harry closed his car door with a slam. He felt a void in his mind of the purest black ice. He already knew what he had to do, but he didn't know if he already wasn't too late. He had miscalculated in his attempt to correct a mistake. When it had happened before, lives had been lost. Never his, always someone close to him.

He had no more emotion. All he had was his body, his mind, and his gun. Before the night was out, he was sure one of them would be empty.

Harry savagely turned his car on, and into gear. He tore around the crippled truck and sped back to the

Berkeley campus. At the same time Lynne McConnell sped away. She wanted to get away. She was willing to risk injury, even death, to escape, but there was nothing she could do. Her hands were cruelly pinned in front of her; her thumbs tied together with wire and thin strips of leather around the driver's waist. Under their jackets were thin belts that further attached them to each other.

Her legs were in leather pants that were laced to the motorcycle itself. And her mouth was filled with a dry sponge which her own saliva was making more sodden all the time. Keeping her from spitting that out was an Ace bandage, wound round and round her head and in between her teeth, secured with several clips. All she could see was the black opaque plastic of the helmet completely covering her head. She did not know what was happening or what had gone wrong.

Harry knew what had gone wrong as he stalked Hinkle down the hall of the Audio Visual Building. Mohamid's ward was not the first room the black man and Tony had visited that morning. It made sense that the slavers had wanted to know how much the cops knew about their operation. The pair of killers had taken a little time, been a little devious, and found out all about the homicide-vice operation to snare The Professor. And the black man, Fish, had probably told them. And Harry had let him go. He wouldn't make the same mistake twice.

As he approached the cellar classroom 27B, he knew he was alone in this thing. He had no solid proof. He was still waiting for a search warrant on Madame's. He couldn't call in the cavalry legally. He knew some would come anyway, but he wouldn't risk their lives as well. One dead and one missing was enough.

Harry pushed open the classroom door. He had seen the flickering light from the otherwise dark classroom at the end of the hall. He heard the same strange soundtrack of heavy breathing, female grunts, and tinkling glass. Harry moved into the room and walked directly in front of the screen, his gun out.

The class moaned as one and started shouting for him to get out of the way. He fired the Magnum once into the ceiling. It was enough to restore order.

"Roy Hinkle," he called simply, the movie playing across his body. "Police business."

"I'm sorry," said a different voice behind the projector. "Mr. Hinkle isn't here tonight. He called in sick. I'm the substitute teacher. Can I . . . uh . . . help you?"

Harry moved away from the screen. The film continued. The substitute teacher was a Mr. Goodwin who didn't know where Hinkle was, didn't know where he lived and hadn't even met the man. Harry moved back to the door.

They were showing *The Bird with the Crystal Plumage* tonight. The last image Harry saw before he left was a man sitting in a chair with a knife in his back and a bloody-faced girl bound and gagged on the floor in front of him.

Chapter Seven

They needed a good one tonight. They had lost the Steinbrunner girl, depleting their shipment by one blond. And, as attractive and expensive as the policewoman was, she was still a brunette. The order specifically called for a natural American blond. The slavers had to get her tonight. They would be forgiven if her background and family ties were not thoroughly checked out this time. After all, it would be their last shipment from San Francisco.

Whatever the final cause for Steinbrunner's escape turned out to be—faulty drugs, inadequate security, or just bad luck—it showed the sign of an eroding organization. The policewoman making the scene was the signing of the group's death certificate. It wasn't wise anyway to take too many women from one area. The organization's success came with relative moderation. Moderation and discerning taste.

Madame's was jumping fairly well for a Monday night. It was a good sign. The scouts on the floor had already spotted three possibilities. It was up to the gentleman to make the final decision. He moved around the crowded dance floor, maintaining the look of a seasoned Lothario. How the girls reacted to his obvious, appraising stare was one of the first barometers of how suitable they would be and how much work it would take to prepare them.

The first blond he came into contact with was of medium height but with huge, thick high heels that could be considered stilts. She whirled around the floor, flinging her long, straight blond hair every which way but loose. She wore a beige leather outfit which hung on her narrow frame. It was slit up the side and cut down to between her tiny breasts. When she twirled, her chest was often exposed, a fact she seemed to acknowledge and revel in. When she caught the gentleman looking at her, she flirted with him unabashedly, putting her arms up like a flamenco dancer, twirling like a maniac, and shouting, "Whoo, whoo, whoo!"

She was an egocentric slut, the gentleman decided. He was glad when he saw strands and roots of black in her lifeless hair. He would have been happy to beat her senseless, but he wouldn't have sold her to anyone.

The second girl was a vast improvement. At least five feet eight inches tall, she was a solid hunk of femininity. She seemed aware of her beauty and did little to call attention to it. It spoke for itself. Through her elegant simplicity, she enhanced her attractiveness twenty fold. She wore an outfit consisting of a maroon leotard, matching wrap skirt, and plain red pumps. Her hair was a flaxen blond, which rolled down the sides of her head in waves, crashing on her shoulders. She returned the gentleman's gaze with demureness. Not looking away immediately, but not inviting anything either. If anything, she was acknowledging. But her eyes were light brown, and that was a bad sign.

The gentleman moved closer. He saw the light brown hair on her arms. It was a dead giveaway. Her yellow head of hair was not natural. The gentleman was disappointed, but he promised himself to find her name at the entry desk in case he ever came back this way again.

He moved on to the last of the early evening choices. He wasn't disgusted as he had been with the first or unduly impressed as he had been with the second, but he smiled to himself. She was pleasing and would be impressive to their buyers. Her golden hair twisted just to the back of her neck. It was cut very well so the disco lights made the ends shine white. She too was fairly tall. At least five-seven, but her body and face were stronger, more muscle than curving adipose tissue. She was, in a word, statuesque.

She wore a handsome black silk-like dress with a deep red floral print across it. It fit her perfectly, from the spaghetti strands over her shoulder to the short slits in the skirt from the top of her calf to the bottom of her thigh. She wore ankle-strap high heels on her feet. She returned the gentleman's gaze intriguingly, then smiled. She was open for suggestion.

The gentleman smiled after she looked away from him. Her eyes had been a clear, light aqua, and her arms were covered with a clear peach fuzz. They had found their blond. Slowly, enjoying the floor show of writhing, disconcerned bodies, the gentleman returned to the disc jockey's booth. The woman and Roy Hinkle were waiting. The gentleman only returned the look of the woman. He nodded at her, holding up three fingers.

The woman checked a chart next to her. "Elizabeth Cook," she read. "Real estate broker."

"Good," said the gentleman. "A career woman. Did you get a readout on her yet?"

"All three reports were made up," replied the woman. "Just in case. Born in November. A Sagittarius. Twenty-two years old. No history of serious ailments. Parents in Nova Scotia."

"That's far enough away," the gentleman commented. "The Canadian environment probably accounts for her health and sturdy build."

"Hmmm," the woman made a positive sound, still pouring over the computer readout. "She seems fine," she finally expressed. "But then we don't have much choice, do we?" She looked pointedly over at Hinkle.

"Is that it?" the teacher asked after a short silence. "What about my suggestions? What about me?"

"Your targets are all on campus," the woman patiently

141

explained. "After all our trouble there we can only hope to take this Miss Cook and get out before it is too late."

"As for you, Professor," the gentleman continued, "you like your women too young. We can use a well-developed prize of fifteen or sixteen . . . it gives the purchases more miles . . . but eleven-year-olds in garbage cans . . . ?"

"I brought you Barbara Steinbrunner," Hinkle pleaded. "Please, I need to get out of the country."

The gentleman and the woman exchanged glances.

"Barbara was an excellent item," he reminded her. "It wasn't The Professor's fault she escaped."

The woman pursed her lips in thought. "Very well," she agreed. "It is easier and cleaner than killing you."

Hinkle breathed an audible and obvious sigh of relief. As nonchalant and unthreatening as the conversation seemed, Hinkle knew his life hung on every word the woman said. She had incredible wealth and power. He had seen her kill people as an afterthought. He knew that she herself had killed men.

"What can I do?" he asked immediately, wanting to show his good intentions.

"Stay here," the woman answered. "Take care of the music. You just have to load each reel as they finish. The two recorders go on and off automatically."

"When should I meet you?" The Professor asked, "and where?"

The woman rose and walked out of the booth without replying. The gentleman followed her, but stopped at the door.

"We'll come for you," he promised, then closed the door behind him.

The pair of slavers strode across the edge of the dance floor toward the office. "What about her date?" the gentleman checked with her, already assuming the answer.

"We can't take chances he'll start an extensive search for her. Now or later. He'll have to die."

The gentleman smiled and nodded. Then they went in the office. It was a simple room with a desk, a file cabinet, and a telephone. The woman sat behind the desk and picked up the phone. The gentleman leaned against the filing cabinet.

The woman called the bartender who was one of the four men who had kidnapped Rose Ray. The bartender listened to his orders, then pressed two buttons under the bar three times, then two times more. Beepers on the belts of the disco's two bouncers—the others beside the bald man who had abducted the black girl—acknowledged the signal with a return beep.

The girl and the plan had been chosen. Elizabeth Cook had been drinking with her boyfriend already. The bartender had already refilled their glasses once. He knew what they were drinking. He waited until one of the three waiters—all of whom were in the Cadillac to disguise Ray's abduction—took another order from them.

He called the office back, then pulled two different pouches from two different slots under the bar. He mixed the couples' drinks then tore open the pouches and poured the contents into their respective glasses. The knowing waiter took the drinks to the couple, who were sitting this dance out.

The gentleman and the woman had moved out of the office. They walked behind the disc jockey booth to a stairway leading to the rest rooms downstairs. The setup was not unusual. The hallway was narrow at the bottom of the steps. One had to take a left to get to the ladies' room on the right wall. Directly across the lavatory door was another door without a knob. Down the hall and to the right was the men's room. The only major difference between this and thousands of other establishments was that the stairs and the men's room hall could be automatically blocked with soundproof partitions. That precaution had never been used.

The gentlemen unlocked the door across from the ladies' room with three keys. He pushed the door open and slipped inside. Seconds later he handed a black rubber face clamp to the woman. She took it by its round, serrated metal grip and went inside the woman's john. The gentleman took up his position on the other side of the metal door. From pegs on the wall behind the portal, he took three pairs of handcuffs, some leather thongs already tied into loose circles and slipknotted, a large red rubber ball attached to a strap that buckled, and a wide leather pad with a sponge covering one side and three thin buckling straps.

He laid the equipment on either side of a padded mat just inside the door opening. Then he stood behind the metal partition, looked through its spy hole, and waited.

Outside, the place was getting busy. The parking attendant had his hands full with cars coming every few seconds. Since it was early in the week, no second man had been hired. The young man was rushing from one auto to another, grabbing keys, taking tips, parking the cars, and rushing back to his post.

It didn't help when the scraped, dark car pulled right by him and parked almost right next to the side of the building. The parking attendant ran over.

"Hey, mister," he told the tall, coarse-faced driver inside. "You can't park there. Come on, let me take your car and put it where it belongs."

The driver looked over and smiled. "Why, thanks," he said, reaching into his tweed jacket. "Here, let me give you a tip."

The parking attendant leaned over. The driver buried his fist in the young man's face.

Inside, Elizabeth Cook had to go to the bathroom. Suddenly the call of nature became overwhelming. She excused herself and went in search of the ladies' room. Her boyfriend just smiled and smiled. She wondered about him. She had only gone out with him once before, but he certainly seemed to be able to hold his liquor then. But tonight, strangely, he had gotten somewhat tipsy on his third glass. Maybe he hadn't eaten. Elizabeth shrugged it off. She had her own pressure to relieve.

She anxiously went down the stairs and around the corner to the rest room. She walked in quickly, ignoring the woman washing at the sink and went right to a stall. Upstairs, the two bouncers moved over to either side of her boyfriend.

"You've had a little too much, buddy," said one. "Time to air out a bit."

The boyfriend just smiled and smiled. He nodded off as the two men grabbed his arms and pulled him out of the seat. They dragged him to the door, nodding at the bartender. The bar man pressed another button. The woman had turned off her beeper but she still saw the flashing light on its top. The gentleman across the hall heard the sound. All clear. Any time. The man checked the bondage instruments a second time. The woman looked down into the sink at the black clamp.

The bouncers dragged the boyfriend out the front of the disco and around to the parking lot. Then they stopped in confusion. The attendant should have heard the signal. He should have had the boyfriend's car waiting for them. Instead, the driveway leading to the main road was empty.

"Fuckin' shithead," the left bouncer declared. "Hold onto this guy. I'll go find him."

The bouncer on the left unwrapped his arm from the semi-conscious boyfriend's shoulder and headed toward the attendant's little booth in the middle of the field. The light inside was on, so he walked right in. The booth was empty. Cursing anew, he walked back to the front of the disco. His fellow bouncer and the boyfriend were gone.

The second bouncer nearly panicked. He was about to run inside to raise an alarm when he heard a groan coming from some bushes at the side of the building. The bouncer relaxed and strode over, complaining.

"Why didn't you tell me you were going to hide him?" the bouncer whined, pushing the shrubbery aside. "I've heard of playing it safe, but this is ridic . . . !"

His sentence was cut off by a big, gnarled hand around his throat and a sledgehammering knee in his balls. His eyes bulged and his face puffed out purple before a second hand grabbed his hair and threw him with the force of a bowling ball against the side of the building. A meaty thunk reverberated along the wood exterior of the disco, then all that could be heard was a rustling of bushes and the crickets.

Elizabeth Cook finished on the toilet. She pulled up her black satin panties, pushed down her dress, flushed, and went out to wash her hands. The woman outside was over by the door with her back toward Cook, seemingly straightening out her outfit. Elizabeth only glanced in her direction before turning her attention to the sink.

She had just turned the water on and wet her hands when the thing slapped over her face. She reared back in surprise, her hands dripping, only to feel the hard shape of someone behind her. Someone who held her around the waist and pushed her head back to rest on that someone's shoulder. Cook had her mouth half open when the horror clamped. Her features froze, her right arm was wrenched up her back and her left arm was grabbed just above the elbow.

She remembered that she had to pull the lavatory door open to get in, so all the woman behind her had to do was propel her forward. Elizabeth slammed by the door, through the hallway, and fell on the mat inside the other door, which the gentleman had opened. The gentleman swung the door shut and pounced on her. It had all happened in five seconds.

The gentleman grabbed one wrist and slapped on one section of the handcuff. He rolled her onto her stomach and slid the other wrist into the metal rope. Her arms were now clinched behind her back. He started cooing while he attached the second pair of handcuffs to her ankles. He dodged her kicking legs like an athlete, then clicked the hitches into place. Her legs were together. He grabbed the last pair of handcuffs in one hand and the short metal chain between the ankle cuffs in the other. He pulled back on the legs, attached one open cuff to the short chain on her wrists and the other to the ankle chain. She lay on her stomach, her knees bent, her high heels almost touching his outstretched fingers behind her back.

The gentleman rolled her on her side and applied both his hands to her stomach. He pushed in hard, then immediately unclamped the thing from her face. It fell away away to reveal Cook's mouth and eyes wide open. The gentleman had knocked the air out of her. She couldn't catch her breath. He filled her mouth with the rubber ball, nimbly buckling it tight behind her head. He pulled her hair from under it and tightened it even more. Only then could she breathe. Her breath exhaled around the

146

obstruction prying her jaws wide open. She moaned in discomfort and confusion.

"Now, now," the gentleman admonished. "Mustn't make any noise." So saying he pressed the sponge end of the leather pad firmly over her opened mouth and the ball, then buckled its ties, all of which fit neatly around the ball buckle. Another thirty seconds had elapsed. The woman walked nonchalantly in, looking down at their helpless captive with satisfaction. They had their blond. The woman signaled the bartender.

The bartender relaxed. He always got a little uptight when they were set to snatch a chick at ground zero. There was so much to watch out for, especially with Tony gone. He had to signal if anyone went downstairs after the targeted prize. He had to keep filling drink orders, and he had to watch out for any undue action on the floor. He was always happiest when it was all over and he knew he had a new toy to play with when he got to the Cave.

The bartender looked over the unusually large Monday crowd. The joint was usually jumping after eleven every night, but here it was hardly ten and the place was packed. He smiled at all the faces that went by. The bartender really enjoyed his work. He felt a special kind of supremacy that only came from knowing you could have any girl you wanted. And not because you were suave or rich, but simply because you wanted her. And there was nothing anyone could do about it.

The bartender was about to be proved wrong. He worked his way down the bar, cleaning the polished surface, chatting with customers, and making drinks. He finally came to the far end, right next to the waiters' station. Two burly guys, probably football players from the college, ordered some brew. The bartender handed them the beer, then twisted his head to the right to take the order of the guy sitting on the bar's last stool. The two ball players went back to their seats, clearing the bartender's sightlines. The guy sitting on the last stool was Harry Callahan.

"I'd like a drink," he said.

The bartender started with surprise. Before he could

move off, Harry grabbed his lapels in both hands and pulled him back.

"I said I'd like a drink," he said dangerously, then added softly, "hands on the bar."

The bartender slowly put his palms flat on the oak surface, nervously looking around all the while. His waiters didn't notice.

"Eyes here," Harry quietly instructed, pointing at the bridge of his nose. "Take it easy. Just keep moving as if nothing is wrong. Make me a drink and talk to me."

"Sure," the bartender smiled widely. "What'll you have?"

"A beer," Harry said. "Where's the girl?"

"What brand?" the bartender answered. "Downstairs."

"What have you got?" Harry continued the charade. "How many with her?"

"Michelob, Miller, Heinekin, Schaeffer, and Becks," the bartender replied to the first question. "Two," he said to the second.

"I'll take a Miller," Harry said simply.

"Light?" the bartender asked.

"No, with all the calories."

The bartender kept smiling, but he didn't move. "Uh," he said, "can I reach down and get it?"

Harry leaned forward and looked at the small freezer on the floor behind the bar. The only buttons he saw were across the room. "OK," he said, "but keep your hands away from the lip."

The bartender knew what he meant. If Harry saw any digit heading toward the underside of the bar, the man had had it. The bartender backed away, keeping a careful smile plastered on his puss. As he expected, Harry remained natural. So natural, in fact, that he glanced at the dance floor for a second.

In that second, the bartender threw open the sliding door on the cooler and pulled out a silenced MAC 11 submachine gun.

Out of the corner of his eye, Harry saw the bartender's quick movement that required the use of two hands. Harry kicked out against the bar, overturning his chair just as the bartender brought up the weapon and pulled the trigger.

Everyone noticed the big guy in the tweed jacket toppling over, but no one seemed to notice the fourteen holes and flying chips of wood that erupted from the bar. The MAC 11 was just a plain black box with a handle and a tube. The hefty silencer completely muffled the reports under the throbbing disco music. It wasn't until Harry brought his feet under him and pulled out the .44 that anyone realized something was very wrong.

Harry blew a hole the size of a quarter through the bar wall. The boom of his Magnum rolled like a wave over the dance floor, stopping everyone in a progressive pattern. His slug swept by the bartender and smashed the mirror behind the bar. It flew out over the bartender and the patrons, throwing off the man's aim and creating a panic.

People began scurrying in every direction. Harry stood straight, his gun pointed directly in front of him. The bartender shook the glass out of his hair. Harry shot him in the chest. The man flew back, his white apron suddenly decorated with red, the MAC 11 flying across the bar and hitting a shocked girl in the side.

Harry kept his gun straight. A waiter ran to the other side of the bar and reached over to hit the console of buttons. Harry shot the black man right between his eyes. The waiter's red blood splashed the backs of patrons scurrying to get out the door. His body fell onto one of the college football boys, who just shouldered him back without looking. What was left of the waiter's head bounced off the edge of the bar.

Harry pivoted as the dance floor cleared. Everyone had pressed away from the bar when the shooting started so the opposite wall of the place looked like a solid throng of terrified cakewalkers. Terrified couples huddled together under tables and in far corners. Harry wasn't interested. He was looking for the other two waiters.

Roy Hinkle leaped up in the disc jockey's booth, panic-stricken before he realized he was behind one-way glass. He wondered whether he should try to warn the gentleman downstairs or whether he should remain safe in the booth. Hinkle, The Professor, sat down. He decided to wait until Callahan was otherwise occupied and then escape with the couple downstairs.

The woman and the gentleman looked up. Naturally the hostage room was soundproof but there was no disguising the difference between dancing and running feet. The two slavers looked at one another with questions in their eyes. Elizabeth simply twisted, turned, and cried on the floor at their feet. The woman buzzed the men upstairs with her beeper. There was no reply.

The waiters were busy. The two men came sweeping out of the office with unsilenced MAC 10s in their hands. These armaments were slightly larger than the 11s, but they were just as deadly. Harry dove over the bar and crashed to the floor behind the beer cooler. The waiters riddled the front of the bar with bullets. Harry heard them thunk and ping through the wood, off the metal, and into the glass. He'd have to do something about them, and quick. The only other difference beween the two MACs was that the 11s were .380 caliber. The 10s were .45. Any closer and the lead would go right through the metal Harry was behind.

Harry reached into the cooler and pulled out a bottle of beer. It was a Heinekin dark mixture. He ripped off the label, pulled off the cap by hand, dug into his pocket for a Kleenex and stuffed it into the open top. He then got on his knees and lobed the bottle toward the dance floor while screaming "Molotov!"

He gave the waiters a second to react, then jumped up. The bluff had worked. As the bottle smashed harmlessly on the thick glass dance floor, Harry shot the waiter to his right. The waiter was cringing away, so the bullet entered his chest from the side, just below his shoulder. He dove sideways from the force of the lead as blood and gore spit out of his other underarm.

Harry was over the bar and running toward a row of couches circling the dance floor. He tried to get the last waiter completely in his sights, but the man was moving too close to the remaining innocent bystanders who hadn't been able to get out any of the doors. Harry dove to the carpet as the waiter realized he had been snookered, slid, and rolled behind the sofa nearest him.

The waiter opened fire and tore the stuffings out of it. But as soon as Harry had landed, he had crawled behind the couch next to that and then the couch after that. The Professor could see what Harry was doing from his vantage point, but the waiter could not. He just kept riddling the same sofa with bullets.

"I'm gonna kill that sucker!" he shouted, laughing.

Hinkle saw his chance. He threw open the booth's door and shouted. "Over there, stupid! He's over there!"

If the circumstances had been a little different, Harry would have taken time to thank the child pornographer. As it was, when the waiter looked back in surprise at Hinkle, Harry shot him in the chest.

It had to be the chest. Only there was enough bone, muscle, and cartilage structure to stop Harry's .44 slug from hitting anyone behind him. The waiter threw his MAC 10 into the air and flew back like a human starfish into the horrified dancers behind him.

Roy Hinkle caught the gun. He grabbed it out of the air at the same time he grabbed a girl dancer by the hair. He pulled the girl in front of him, wrapped his arm around her neck, and stuck the muzzle of the MAC against her temple.

"That's it, Callahan," he said, pulling the girl back toward the booth. "It's over. Put your gun down."

In reply, Harry stood up, his gun still out before him.

"Come on, Callahan," The Professor taunted, keeping his head behind the statuesque blond. It was the second girl the gentleman had scouted. Hinkle had chosen her for her proximity and height. "I count one bullet left in your gun. Do you think you can nail me with that one bullet? Are you that good? Or are you going to blow this little lady's head apart? Or plug one of the people behind me? What do you say, Callahan? Do you feel lucky?"

By then, The Professor was close enough. He jumped back into the disc jockey's booth pulling the girl with him. He slammed the door behind him and turned the music all the way up.

The noise on the dance floor was nearly unbearable.

Everyone slapped their hands over their ears and crawled away from the blaring speakers. Harry used his last bullet to smash the amplifier nearest him. He was about to empty the shells and shove in an auto-loader when a .45 bullet bore through the booth's one-way glass and nicked Harry's ear.

Harry dropped behind the couch, his revolver still open. That miserable son of a bitch was shooting at him from behind the safety of both one-way glass and a hostage. He knew Harry couldn't shoot back blindly for fear of hitting the girl. And now The Professor knew that his weapon, kept on single fire, would only put a hole in the glass, not shatter it. He could see Harry, but Harry couldn't see him.

The cop quickly reloaded his gun. He looked in every direction. People were painfully groveling away from the cacophony of the thundering disco music. The bass beat alone seemed to be shaking the entire building. He located another speaker above him and shot it out. There was one by the bar. He rolled over and shot that too. Now the noise was just about bearable. He looked around at the cowering patrons inside the disco.

"Get out!" he shouted. "He doesn't want you! Go on, get out of here!"

Needing only that permission, the revelers moved back toward the exits. While they slowly filed out, Harry grabbed the bottom of the sofa and tipped it over. As it fell forward, another bullethole appeared in the booth's glass and plunked deep into the couch seat. Harry moved forward a bit more. Then he repeated the action. The sofa fell a bit closer to the booth. Another bullethole appeared. The slug blew off the bottom of an upturned wooden leg on the furniture.

With one more push, Harry got the sofa all the way to the dance floor. Any farther and Hinkle could hit him from his perspective. Harry lay behind the couch and found the remaining four speakers. He shot out two of them. The music was still playing, but it continued only in regular stereo. Without the din, Harry could think again.

To compensate for the lack of disco beat, Hinkle started dotting the sofa with bullets in a regular rhythm.

Every other second another hole would appear somewhere on the glass and another slug would rip through the couch. It was just a matter of time before they found a human target.

Harry saw one tear up a hunk of wood from the dance floor right between his legs. He knew it was time to move on to other cover. He quickly looked to the side. There was an overturned table not three yards from him. But those three yards looked a lot longer from where he was lying.

Another bullet whined off an innerspring and shot out of the upholstery not a inch from his head. It was time to move. Harry was steeling to cover himself when he remembered the blond in the maroon bodysuit. He couldn't shoot back into the booth, but that didn't mean he couldn't shoot at all.

Harry turned over onto his stomach and got up in the start position for a race. He held his Magnum pointed toward the booth. He leaped forward and shot at the same time. It just barely worked. His bullets whacked into the ceiling over the booth, but that didn't keep Hinkle from returning the fire. The edge of the couch ripped open and then the bullets trailed Harry's movements like a faithful dog. The cop stopped behind the table, but the bullets kept going.

They smashed into the tabletop in a wavy line, some embedding deep in the thick wood, others ramming through. But since Harry was flat on his back, they went over his head. Even the hostage situation had its positive aspects, Harry realized. At least holding the girl as a shield screwed up Hinkle's aim.

Harry exhaled mightily while emptying his second set of shells. He placed his third auto-loader in and he looked up at the ceiling to see what damage he'd done. His bullets had blown out a light and nicked the tube that was holding the mirror ball steady above the dance floor. Harry smirked in spite of his predicament. Every disco had to have its mirror ball. The bigger the disco, the bigger the mirror ball. Madame's had a huge one.

Harry halted his derision. He spun over onto his side and hazarded a glance at the booth. Another bullet hole appeared as he watched. He snapped his head back. But it was enough. He saw that the one-way glass was thoroughly dotted with holes. And off of most of these holes were tiny cracks. They weren't enough to shatter the cover, but one large push might be enough to do it. A .44 bullet couldn't do the job, but a reflecting wrecking ball could.

Callahan studied the mirror ball above him. There was the rod in the top which turned it around. And there were four wires holding the rod steady. One wire going in each direction. Harry had six shots. He had to do it with five and he couldn't do it from directly under the ball.

Clamping his jaw together and grinding his teeth, Harry grabbed onto the table's one thick center leg with his left arm. He tightened his grip on the Magnum in his right hand. He pulled his feet under him.

Harry stood up, took two steps back, and started firing.

He held the table in front of him like a medieval shield as he kept all his attention on the mirror ball's wires. He heard and felt Hinkle's shots flying around him. One shot, the west wire snapped. Two shots, the south wire broke. Three shots, the east wire was cut. A .45 bullet smashed against the side of his shoe. His foot went numb, his leg shifted, and the fourth shot went wild.

Harry almost fell. He almost dropped the table. He yanked his body straight again and with his lips pulling off his teeth, he aimed the gun at the already nicked tube. The mirror ball was already spinning wildly in every direction, throwing thousands of rectangular light beams across the walls and floors. Every time Harry thought he had the tube lined up, a light beam would flash in his eyes and the aim was off again.

Inside the booth, Hinkle hurled the girl away from him in frustration. Weak from fear, the blond hit the side wall and slipped to the floor. The Professor took the MAC 10 in both hands and tried to level Harry where he stood. The .45 bullets drilled out the glass into the very edge of the table shield.

Harry felt the table buck in his hands and actually saw the bullets ricochet over his head. Then he fired the fifth shot.

The tube broke. The north wire held, swinging the big, glittering ball right at the disc jockey's booth.

The destruction of the glass was extraordinary. The mirrored ball broke open like a shattering water balloon, sending hundreds of spinning little squares off like the rays from the sun. Even more of the mirror powdered, spreading a sparkling gray cloud across the disc jockey booth's protection.

At first it didn't seem as if the one-way pane would give, but as the gray cloud dissipated, hunks of light broke through. The booth's glass fell in like pieces of a jigsaw puzzle falling from the ceiling. They all shattered on the burnished wood and lighted glass dance floor with a crackling roar.

Harry dropped the table as The Professor was forced back. He stumbled toward the girl. Harry shot him in the back. Hinkle was thrown forward, his arms limp behind him. His face hit the wall above the girl. Harry didn't wait for him to crumble. He charged right by the booth and pounded downstairs, reloading his Magnum as he went.

He nearly slammed face first into a steel curtain that blocked the bottom of the staircase. A sign on it read, "We are sorry, but the rest rooms are out of service at this time."

Harry cursed and ran back to the bar. Reaching over the edge, he pressed down all the buttons. As he ran back, he saw the captive blond carefully making her way out of the booth. He wanted to help her, but he had more pressing matters to attend to.

This time the stairway was clear. Harry kicked open the ladies' room door. Empty. He kicked at the door across the hall. It wouldn't budge. He blasted away at the lock with his .44 until it fell completely out of the metal partition and clattered on the floor. Harry hurled it inward.

The room wasn't empty, but there were no people inside. Instead there was equipment. There were four tables lined with the most incredible array of restraining devices Harry had ever seen. The tables themselves had straps to hold the entire body still. There was rope, leather cord, wire and tape of all shapes and sizes. There were handcuffs, padlocks, and chains. And that was just in the middle of the floor.

To his left was a complete makeup center with wigs, every type of cosmetic imaginable, and a full paint set. On the back wall was a lab stocked with drugs. And to his right was a large computer. The information section of the unit was as big as a casket. The readout and keyboard were the same sort one would find in any modern newsroom. Harry turned on the power. A flashing green star immediately appeared in the upper left hand corner of the screen. Harry typed in Lynne McConnell's name. He hit the "Enter" button.

Her name flashed on the screen twice, then records began to march up the screen like the cast and credits of a TV show. The machine displayed her birth certificate, some school report cards, her driver's license, her bank statements, her college diploma, her tax form, hospital records, her life insurance policy, and even the lease on her apartment.

Harry switched off the computer without emotion. He ran back upstairs and hopped into the disc jockey's booth. Hinkle was where he had shot him. Harry gingerly turned him over. The Professor was leaking blood from his nose and mouth as well as his back.

"Get 'em?" Hinkle asked softly.

"Long gone," said Harry.

Hinkle chuckled and a renewed stream of crimson drooled out of the corners of his mouth.

"Figures," he finally said, grimacing with the pain.

"Save the death scene," Harry stated. "If you know where they went, say so."

The Professor thought about all the ironies of life. He thought about how there was no honor among thieves. He thought about his life and felt no remorse for the things he did. He felt no regret that he had ended this way either. But all he said was, "Angel Island. House on the Northern face. Call it the Cave."

Harry didn't thank him. He just got up and started to walk away.

"Hey," Hinkle said.

Harry turned.

The Professor smiled a death smile. The blood had tained his teeth. It was a smile that said Harry didn't have a chance. "Do you feel lucky, Callahan?" he asked. Then he lowered his head to the floor and died.

Harry looked at the corpse in the devastated disco for a few seconds.

"That's my line," he told the body. "Punk."

Chapter Eight

It was nearly midnight when Harry arrived on Angel Island. He had had to drive all the way to Fisherman's Wharf to find a cruiser captain still up and about. The tour boats were supposed to stop running at four o'clock in the afternoon, but a police badge and a loaded Magnum went a long way in loosening the moorings. Fifty bucks started the engine and raised the anchor.

Harry jumped off the salt-eaten deck onto a crumbling cement jetty on the north side of the island.

"There it is," said Orville, the crusty little seahorse who had brought him this far. "The Cave."

Harry looked up at the dark, foreboding mansion overlooking the Raccoon Strait.

"People call it that because they figger a whole system of caves runs underneath it," Orville explained. "People figger a whole horde of gold was hidden in 'em after the rush of 1849." The old man squinted up at the house himself. "Great earthquake probably destroyed 'em, though." He shook his head. "Want me to wait?" he asked Harry.

"No," Callahan answered. "Thanks."

"Okie-doke," Orville said, figuring the cop knew what he was doing.

Harry was already marching through the brush toward the mansion by the time the captain had cast off. He pulled out his weapon when the shadow of the place blotted out the moon.

It was another world here. A world of gothic horror, of dark despair, where the worst nightmares of a society trying to become liberated came true. Harry still had no proof. He had a disco full of terrified dancers and dead bodies but no real, prosecutable proof. He had a cellar that would set a sadist's heart aflame, but he had no corroborating witnesses. Just a well-programmed computer and a lot of *corpus delecti*.

There were two more in the cellar with the girl, the bartender had said. Two more in the cellar, Harry thought, and how many more here? He soon got his answer. He heard a sound behind him and to his right. He spun around, his gun cocked.

It was Orville, the boat man, coming up to him and holding out a flashlight. "Here," he said, flicking it on, "I thought you might need this. . . ."

As soon as the light went on the night was torn open by the rasping growl of a submachine gun. Harry saw the captain's middle get torn open by the bullets. He threw himself back and down as the poor old man and the flashlight dropped.

The only noise for seconds after that was the sound of the flashlight rolling down the hill toward the jetty. Harry watched the dot of white light get smaller and smaller until it smashed against a rock. The noise continued but the light went out. Finally the noise stopped too.

"I think I got him," a voice said.

"Yeah, me too," said another. "Come on."

Harry kept perfectly still as two men, armed with G3 assault rifles, sidled up to the dead man.

"That's him, huh?" the first one said, prodding the corpse with his toe. "He doesn't look like much."

The other shrugged. "Ours is not to reason why. . . ." he quoted.

Harry couldn't resist. "Yours is just to do and die," he said. Callahan really wasn't taking too much of a chance finishing the sentence because as he spoke, he blew both men away so fast his Magnum reports sounded as one.

The men spun and flew back, their rifles following the flashlight down the hill.

Harry had no time to mourn the old sea salt's meaningless murder. He ran up the remainder of the hill to the mansion, flattening against the nearest windowless wall he saw. Up close, the place wasn't much different than it was from far away. The night hadn't masked any windows, he noted, because there were no windows to mask. The whole side of the building had no opening. Harry walked around to the back of the house, away from the side that faced the strait.

There was one door back there, and in front of that door was the black man Harry knew as Fish. The black looked with trepidation in all directions, but he didn't see Harry until the barrel of the .44 touched his neck.

"You've got a big mouth," Harry told him, then brutally flung him against the wall. He bounced back toward Harry, who pushed him again. He kicked Fish's legs wide, threw his arms up, and frisked him as Fish pleaded.

"Hey, man, they were going to kill me. I swear, they had my fucking head over a stove. I couldn't help it, man. What did you want me to do?"

Harry spun him around, pinned his neck to the wall with one hand, and pressed the Magnum against his temple with the other. "Die," he said.

"No, no wait!" the black man screamed. Harry tapped him lightly on his Adam's apple. Fish choked on his begging and fell to his knees.

"Keep your voice down," Harry ordered. He grabbed him by the Afro and pulled him to his feet again. "Now what will you do to stay alive?"

"I can bring you to her, man," Fish whispered.

"Who?"

"The woman, jack. The boss. The head honcho."

"And how many others?" Harry snarled.

"No, no, c'mon, man," the black man pleaded, trying to twist his head out of Harry's grip. "There's nobody

161

left. You got them all. It's just her now, waiting for the ship to come in."

"Isn't everybody?" Harry grinned mirthlessly, digging his fingers deeper into the black man's Afro.

"I swear," Fish begged. "It's the slaver's ship, man! You catch her with that and you'll have it all wrapped up."

Harry suddenly let him go. They stood opposite each other at a distance of five feet. Harry held the gun steady on a level with his chest. There wasn't much more to be made of the situation. Either he killed Fish or he didn't. If he did, he was back on his own. If he didn't, even if Fish led him into a trap, he'd be inside. Closer to McConnell.

Harry pictured her face. "All right," he told the black man. "Let's go."

With great relief, Fish easily opened the plain wooden door and walked inside. As Harry followed him he noticed the inside part of the door was solid steel. They entered a deteriorating front parlor, all cracking cement and tarnished marble. The most notable feature of the room was the two marble columns near the center. Columns that stretched from the once sumptuous floor to the ceiling, now peeling, twelve feet above. Flickering candles were all over the place.

Fish walked between the columns to the entrance of a long hallway. There were open rooms to either side of the passage, their doors either hanging off their hinges or gone completely. The pair walked through without incident. But as they walked, Harry noticed the black man's pace quickening. As if he was tired of the whole affair and anxious to have it end.

At the end of the hall, the way narrowed somewhat. The number of rooms multiplied, and the air was thick with wax smoke from the candles. Harry's eyes began to smart. In the gloom of the long, winding passageways, Harry thought of another reason they called it the Cave. Moving through the oppressive dimness Harry thought about his long afternoon and evening of trying to find McConnell. He had killed them all to reach her. He thought he had almost found her at the disco, but he let her slip through his fingers. She was down with the other two, the bartender had said.

Two . . . ? Fish had said that only the woman was left!

Harry saw Fish almost ten feet ahead of him. He looked at the walls as he passed them. They were beige plaster, reinforced with intermittent wood beams. Thin, crumbling plaster. He looked ahead. They were coming to a small section of hall up three steps. The walls were even closer together than before. Three people could hardly pass shoulder to shoulder. And Fish was ten feet ahead.

The black man took the steps all in one jump. Harry was right behind him. He heard a scrape to his right and saw the peephole just as he grabbed Fish by the back of the neck. When it happened, it happened fast.

Callahan wrenched Fish in front of him as a machine-gun blast tore through the plaster wall. The black man caught it full in the chest. Harry pushed his Magnum between Fish's dying torso and arm and shot point-blank into the peephole. Blood sloshed through the tears in the plaster.

But it wasn't over. Harry heard another peephole slide back behind him and to his left. He hurled Fish down the steps and threw himself back against the wall. Machine-gun bullets poured out of the wall next to him. They tore off the edge of the beam he was behind, but the killer couldn't bring the gun far enough to the right to peg him.

Harry crouched, leaned out, and shot up into the wall. The bullets stopped coming from that section. Harry glanced to his right. There was another peephole two beams down from the first one. Harry had the system now. Four assassins, two on either side of the hall, staggered in rooms behind the wall so they wouldn't catch each other in crossfires. The rooms must have been built in the heyday of the gold rush to discourage thieves and swindlers.

Harry rolled down the passage and came up to the left of the peephole in the right wall. He saw another hole and heard a gun bolt click back right in front of him. He fired at the center of the left wall just as bullets spat out of the right wall beside him. Harry pressed the .44 barrel against the right wall, right over the peephole, and fired his last bullet.

He ran to the end of the hall and down the other steps, dumping his empty shells and reloading in two seconds flat. There was a door on either side. He kicked the left one open first. There was one dead man with a gaping wound in his chin and another crawling around the room on his back, trying to hold his intestines in. Harry ran across to the other door and shouldered it open. Two more corpses. A Magnum slug in one chest and another in a forehead. The flies had already set up housekeeping.

Harry stood at the end of the hallway, looking at the beige plaster flecked with red and the torn-up corpse of the black man known as Fish. He turned when he heard the scream.

The hall emptied out onto a circular room with a domed ceiling. The scream's echo seemed to come from everywhere. It sounded again, narrowing the field to a large wooden door set deep in the stone wall of the room. Harry grabbed the heavy metal ring set in the middle of the portal and pulled. Slowly, the thick door swung back with a painful creak. Inside was a descending staircase of stone steps.

At first, Harry's weariness and the flickering candlelight combined to make him feel as if he had stumbled back into history or onto a film set. The winding stairwell finished up in a subterranean dungeon. There were shackles set in rings on the walls. A broken rack in a heap in the corner. A gibbet, used for displaying dead bodies, hung from the ceiling. It was the ancient equivalent of the hostage room at the disco.

And in the center of the antiquated torture chamber was a woman. A naked woman locked in a fetal position on her back by one of the rusted metal instruments. It was all one piece, a long metal bar that wrapped around the back of her neck then moved down between her legs. Another two bands were attached to the outside of the bar, clamping her wrists to the main bar, then moving down on the outside of her legs. Each bar ended with a circle of iron so another, shorter bar could be thrust through the holes to keep the bonds in place. Finally, two horseshoe-shaped shackles were attached to the short bar to keep the ankles trapped and the thighs pressed against the stomach.

The archaic device was keeping the woman in agony. She screamed again. Harry noticed the loose kerchief around her neck and the wet rolled-up handkerchief lying next to her head. By the looks of it, she had been able to loosen her gag and cry for help.

"Take it easy," Harry told her, holding his hand over her mouth. "We can't have anyone else rushing in." He saw the one padlock holding the short and the two long bars together. Knowing it was the only way, Harry put his gun as close as he could to the lock and shot it off.

The woman hissed as the Magnum's flash and recoil sizzled against her calves. But within seconds, Harry had loosened the device and pulled the woman free. She grabbed him around the neck and sobbed.

The woman's weight was keeping him off balance. He tried to get up, but her hysterical grip was surprisingly strong. He had to let go off his gun to gently unwrap her arms from his neck. As soon as he had gotten free, the woman had fallen over on her side, away from him, still sobbing.

Harry stood, marveling at the viciousness of the case. He leaned on a chopping block next to him, fingering an iron mask, wondering how a woman could do such nasty things to other women. He wondered where the woman— the head honcho the late Fish had called her—was.

Then all of a sudden, he knew. And it was the woman's inexperience with the Magnum and Harry's immediate reaction that saved his life.

He twisted around the chopping block just as the naked woman fired. The bullet sliced across Harry's ear, deafening him for a second. The big gun bucked in her hand, pointing at the ceiling. Despite a loud ringing in his ears, Harry managed to swing the iron mask around and bat the revolver out of her hand. The Magnum soared across the room, bounced across the floor, and clattered against the wall.

It didn't stop the woman for a second. She reached behind her and pulled a huge, two-pronged boat hook of its ring on the wall. She swung it at Harry with a speed that rivaled any man he had faced. Harry parried with the iron mask. One thick point rang off the heavy effigy sending up sparks. She swung back. Harry dodged and swung his own weapon. It glanced off her shoulder. She shrugged it off.

The two antagonists separated and faced each other warily from across the torture chamber. When she wasn't bent double, Harry could see that she was a tall, muscular woman with streaked hair that came to just below her ears. In her bare feet, in her bare body, she still looked to be close to six feet tall. She had no breasts to speak of and while all women were supposed to have ten percent more adipose tissue than men, Harry couldn't find it on her. She was all coiled hemp muscles, coarse hair, and glistening sweat.

"Madame, I presume?" Harry asked.

The woman guardedly nodded, letting a grim smile spread her lips. She moved back toward the gun.

Harry ran around to block her. She feinted to the right, moved in, and swung the hook in a fast, vicious arc. Harry almost fell for it again. The hook smashed into the iron mask that Harry hastily raised, split it open, and wrested it from his grasp. Callahan spun, grabbed the bars the woman had been trapped in and held those up as a shield.

"And you're Dirty Harry," the naked woman said, not even breathing heavily. "You're not very smart, Inspector."

"But I'm very hard to kill," he answered, moving back.

"What?" the woman asked. "Afraid of a woman?"

"Wouldn't you be?" Harry said, still moving back. "Looked in the mirror lately?" He stepped forward, swinging the bar down over his head. The woman parried by lifting the hook effortlessly, pulling the bar out of Harry's still-burned hands. The bar clanged into the hanging gibbet, setting it rocking back and forth with an ugly creak.

Harry backed up to the wall, and the woman moved in

with the hook up over her shoulder. She brought it down to sink into his face, but Harry slid down the wall and grabbed the hooks right behind the points. He straightened and pushed back. He underestimated the woman's strength. She held firm, then tried to knee him in the groin. He blocked that with his thigh, but then the woman pulled up on the hook with all her might, wrenching it from Harry's weak grip and catching him under the chin.

Harry looked through the purple splotches that colored his vision for a second, put his foot in her stomach, and kicked out. She dropped the hook and fell over the chopping block. Harry picked up the hook in one hand. The naked woman got to her feet with a headman's axe. It had been under the block all the time.

The adversaries stood facing each other.

"What do you get out of it?" Harry asked.

"I love it!" the woman roared. "Do you have any idea how easy it is? Out of the hundreds of millions of people in this country alone, do you know how many pretty girls there are? And out of them, how many with loose parental ties and no steady boyfriends? Do you know how many could simply disappear without anyone really noticing?"

"And the computer finds them," Harry filled in.

"My husband is an expert," she bragged. "He calls the different machines up, plays a different code to each one over the phone, sets a hook-up, and these things just spill their guts!"

"Your husband?"

"The Gentleman," the woman elaborated, "as the girls are wont to call him. No names, please. We gave ours up seven years ago."

Harry was legitimately stunned. "How many girls have you taken?"

"Not many," the woman shrugged. "Eight, maybe ten a year. After a while we filled specific orders. Once the oil crisis and U.S. auto sales plummeted, the Arab and Oriental nations were eager to buy what we were selling. We supply only the best to the best."

"That your motto?" Harry suggested sarcastically.

"Shame, shame, Inspector Callahan," the woman admonished. "Our girls are treated very well by their own ers. They are rich enough and powerful enough to keep them very happy or very quiet. It is the girl's choice."

"Not here. Not tonight."

"Well, that is all your fault, Inspector. We had the situation well in hand until you became involved. And after you are gone, we'll relax for a while with our accumulated wealth."

"It couldn't buy you better security," Harry reminded her, motioning his head upstairs to the fly-ridden corpses in the ambush hallway.

"We get by," the woman sniffed. "We never utilize a large staff. The less mouths, the better security. We only use as many as we need to control the supply. Tonight is our biggest shipment in some years. Five million dollars worth."

Harry's mind raced furiously. It was tonight. Fish hadn't lied about that. But how many more guards were there? And where were they? "Five million!" Harry exclaimed aloud, letting a look of surprise flash over his features. "How many girls do you have now?"

"Just three," the woman confessed. "A natural blond, a liberated black, and the policewoman." The woman frowned. "The blond and your friend make up the bulk of the package. Negroes are not in great demand in the Middle East. But we can probably unload her in Japan or China."

The woman sighed and set her footing, waving the axe from side to side. "But I could talk to you all night, Inspector," she said. "It's so rare that I actually get to talk about all this. You know how it is. After a hard day at work, your loved ones don't want to talk shop."

And after that, the woman raced in, swinging the axe with an athletic grace. Callahan wasn't used to the awkward weapons, and his hands were stiff after the tense action of the last few hours. He successfully blocked the new attack, but he couldn't get under her offense.

She whirled like a dervish, slamming the axe blade against the double-pointed hook with increasing force. She kept moving forward, flailing the axe in dazzling geometric patterns. Harry couldn't get away from it. She pushed him back up against the wall, then ran backward, laughing.

"Come on," she urged him forward. "Come on, Inspector. Don't let a woman beat you. Come on."

Harry looked across the room at his gun. It was way beyond reach. He looked at the littered floor of the dungeon. He saw the iron mask she had knocked open with one swipe of her arm. He saw the shadows of something inside. Harry looked at the hook in his hands. He saw his hands were vibrating. The strain of the fight was becoming too much. He dropped the hook and walked purposely forward.

The woman looked at him approaching empty-handed for a moment with disbelief, then she swung back the axe blade with a delighted look on her face. "Don't think I won't," she warned.

Harry kept coming.

She grinned with all her teeth showing and lunged forward, the axe already slicing through the air.

Harry simply dropped beneath the blade, scooped up the iron mask, rose up behind her swinging arms, and slammed it on her face.

The shadows inside the mask had been those of spikes that pointed inward throughout the device.

The woman's scream was real this time and horrible as the spikes drove through her lower lip, both cheeks, an eye and her forehead. She tried to swing the axe back, but Harry was too close to her. He blocked the free movement of her arms. Grimacing, he grabbed the back of her head and pushed with both arms. The mask sunk in farther.

Blood spurted out the mask's macabre eye holes and breathing slits. For a second, it looked like the metal face was crying crimson tears. Harry kept pushing until the woman was bent over backward on the chopping block.

Harry reached down to the other side of the mask, the back of the head portion. As he grabbed its edge, he felt some spikes on that side too. His lips curled up from his teeth like a wolf in blood frenzy. He slammed the mask

169

completely shut. The woman's body jerked on top of the chopping block. She fell over to the floor, the mask slipping out of Harry's hands and partially loosening from her head.

Harry retrieved the padlock he had shot off the woman's initial bonds. He saw that the bottom lock section was ruined, but the top clasp was still intact. He reached down dispassionately and slipped it through the two circles on the outside of the mask. He then jammed it in place.

And still the woman wasn't dead. She squirmed around the floor on her back like a spider with half its legs cut off. Or a worm cut in two.

Harry picked up his gun. It felt solid in his hand. The weight was what was needed. The shakiness subsided and disappeared. Harry walked up the steps slowly, ignoring the naked woman with the steel head and the mane of liquid red.

Harry retraced his steps, picking up one of the G3 assault rifles as he went. Most of the candles had died so he was cautious but not unduly so. He made it out the back door and trotted to the side of the house facing Raccoon Strait.

Sure enough, down the hill, there in the moonlight, was a dock. On the dock were three boxes. Harry moved down warily, waiting for any sudden move any leftover guards might make. Nothing happened; he arrived at the port of call without incident. He put the gun in its holster and ripped the first box open with his bare hands.

Inside was a striking blond girl with her arms wrapped around her waist, each hand in a thumbless leather mitten that tightened around her wrists and was attached to the other hand by an unbreakable wire behind her back. Her legs were bent by a strap that attached each ankle to the very top of each of her thighs. The bottom of her face was completely covered by a roll of Ace bandages.

Harry moved to the second box. Inside was Rose Ray. She was lying on her side, her arms held behind her by a single glove that laced all the way up to her shoulders. Her legs were encased similarly in a single black boot. Her mouth was covered with wide strips of silver tap

170

that reached up to the bridge of her nose and then underneath her chin for mooring.

The third box held McConnell. Her wrists were tied to her thighs. Her ankles were tied to each side of the box. Her head was completely covered by a black hood that tightened around her neck. Harry pulled that off. He pulled off the strap over her eyes. He pulled off the cotton balls stuck to her eyelids. He undid the knot tied between her teeth. Then he pulled a sopping wet sack from her mouth. All three women were naked and all three were unconscious.

Harry looked down at Lynne McConnell. She slept in a heavy drug-induced stupor. But her face was serene. Callahan only hoped he had harassed the slavers too much. He hoped they only had had time to get her to the Cave, then go out to Madame's for the night. He hoped they only had had time to stuff the women in these crates before he showed up.

Harry wondered what it felt like to be meat. To be worthless. To mean nothing. It must be horrible, he calmly considered. Life would become nothing more than a long death.

"I give up, Inspector," Harry heard a quiet, soothing voice say behind him.

He turned around in the early morning darkness, moonlight reflecting off the water, making the whole environment a deep, calming blue. He saw a man who could only be The Gentleman, also known as Rose Ray's "lawyer," standing across the dock with his hands in his pockets.

"You have won, I see," he continued serenely. "We have tried to stop you at every turn, but you have emerged triumphant. So I will go quietly. I figure it is Kismet. You know?"

The man must've known his wife was dead. But any man who could do what he did could not have seen anyone, even his wife, as a real human being.

"Did you do this?" Harry motioned to the boxes.

"We could not let the . . . uh, *them* raise a fuss if they were to awaken prematurely."

"The ship doesn't know what it is delivering then?"

"Oh no," The Gentleman said.

Harry nodded, looked down at McConnell, then pulled out his Magnum, and pointed it at The Gentleman.

The slaver's eyes widened, his hands went out in a pleading pose, and Harry blew his balls off.

Everything between The Gentleman's legs tore out along with sections of his cream-colored slacks and clean underwear. The mutilated package flew across the surface of the water, skipped, splashed, and then sank.

The Gentleman fell to his knees, his hands trying to stop the flow of gore out of the hole between his legs. He looked at the guts spilling over his hands, shrieked once, defecated, and fell forward.

Dirty Harry Callahan untied all the women and left them sleeping peacefully under the boxes' packing. He looked out at the water and considered washing his demons away in it. Instead, he kicked off his shoes, rolled up his pant legs and sat on the edge of the dock.

He put the G3 rifle across his knees and waited for the ship to arrive.

MEN OF ACTION BOOKS
NINJA MASTER
By Wade Barker

The Ninja Master is Brett Wallace, San Francisco partner in the hottest Japanese restaurant in town and a martial-arts studio. He marries a beautiful Japanese woman and begins to take over his father's real-estate business—when tragedy strikes. His pregnant wife and parents are savagely murdered by a hopped-up motorcycle gang—and the killers escape justice when their case is thrown out of court on a technicality.

Revenge becomes Wallace's career. He brings his own form of justice to the killers and then escapes to a secret Ninja camp in Japan to become a master in the deadly craft. Armed with a new identity, he roves the world bringing justice to people who have been wrongfully harmed and whom the legal system has failed. From slavers in South Africa to bizarre religious cults to the Chinese Mafia, the Ninja Master is feared and revered as he combines a talent for modern justice with an ancient art of killing.

NINJA MASTER #1: VENGEANCE IS HIS
(C30-032, $1.95)
NINJA MASTER #2: MOUNTAIN OF FEAR
(C30-064, $1.95)
NINJA MASTER #3: BORDERLAND OF HELL
(Coming in February) (C30-127, $1.95)

HE'S UNSHAKABLE, UNSTOPPABLE, UNKILLABLE...
CAPTAIN GRINGO

RENEGADE #1
by Ramsay Thorne   (C90-976, $1.95)

He's a man on the run—Captain Gringo. By wit, by guile, by masterful skill with guns and women, he'll burn his way across the Border—wiping out a troop of Rurales and the sadistic pervert who commands them, leading a guerilla band on daredevil raids, hijacking, fighting, killing, winning.

RENEGADE #2: BLOOD RUNNER
by Ramsay Thorne   (C90-977, $1.95)

They're waiting for a man like Captain Gringo in Panama! Every adventurer with a scheme, every rebel with a cause wants a man like Captain Gringo—running guns, unloosing a rain of death from his Maxim, fighting Yellow Jack, Indians, army ants, even the Devil himself if he stands in the way!

RENEGADE #3: FEAR MERCHANT
by Ramsay Thorne   (C90-761, $1.95)

In this revolution-wracked land, no one can be trusted. With his eyes wide open and his Maxim at the ready, the Captain is primed for action: in the bed of a Chinese girl, at the challenge of a one-eyed general, at the command to murder a high-born lady, at the demand for love in the savage stare of an Indian girl.

RENEGADE #4: DEATH HUNTER
by Ramsay Thorne   (C90-902, $1.95)

In these cool and quiet nights Captain Gringo trails the highlands with his profile low and his Maxim ready. It's been a year of hell fighting his way through three revolutions and a U.S. courtmartial. But before Captain Gringo's vacation ends, he will have a job—masterminding an attack on three of the world's major powers!

HE'S UNSHAKABLE, UNSTOPPABLE, UNKILLABLE, CAPTAIN GRINGO

RENEGADE #5: MACUMBA KILLER
by Ramsay Thorne   (C90-234, $1.95)

On this sweltering, voo-doo crazed island, the British Empire is breathing its last, subject to the forays of a marauding army of runaways and doped-up derelicts who have unleashed a reign of terror, death, and destruction. The British need a man to take charge, shoot straight, and spit in the enemy's eye—Captain Gringo is that man.

RENEGADE #6: PANAMA GUNNER
by Ramsay Thorne   (C90-235, $1.95)

Captain Gringo's trapped aboard a crippled gunboat in shark-infested waters. Sudden mutiny on the part of Gringo's crew just adds to his inconvenience, but what's really playing havoc with the Captain's mind is the inexplicable interest he's feeling in a young, red-haired kid named Mac.

RENEGADE #7: DEATH IN HIGH PLACES
by Ramsay Thorne   (C90-548, $1.95)

Captain Gringo is leading a brigade through a maze of volcanoes whose molten lava fills the trail, while the burning sting of the common fly sets the pace. Colombia is a political powder keg, and he's bound for Bogota to light the fuse that will ignite an explosion of chaos, destroying the country's corrupt and depraved regime.

RENEGADE #8: OVER THE ANDES TO HELL
by Ramsay Thorne   (C90-549, $1.95)

There's no rest for Gringo in Bogota. Between seduction in the eyes of the senoritas and murder in the minds of the Kaiser's spies, a man has to keep moving to stay alive. From the hot Amazon jungle thick with headhunters to the chilling Andes rife with rebels, the Captain is on a trek to trouble.

6 EXCITING ADVENTURE SERIES
MEN OF ACTION BOOKS
FROM WARNER BOOKS

DIRTY HARRY
by Dane Hartman
#1 DUEL FOR CANNONS   (C90-793, $1.95)
#2 DEATH ON THE DOCKS   (C90-792, $1.95.

THE HOOK
by Brad Latham
#1 THE GILDED CANARY   (C90-882, $1.95.
#2 SIGHT UNSEEN   (C90-841, $1.95

S-COM
by Steve White
#1 THE TERROR IN TURIN   (C90-992, $1.95,
#2 STARS AND SWASTIKAS   (C90-993, $1.95,

BEN SLAYTON: T-MAN
by Buck Sanders
#1 A CLEAR AND PRESENT DANGER (C30-020, $1.95)
#2 STAR OF EGYPT   (C30-017, $1.95)

NINJA MASTER
by Wade Barker
#1 VENGEANCE IS HIS   (C30-032, $1.95)
#2 MOUNTAIN OF FEAR   (C30-064, $1.95)

BOXER UNIT—OSS
by Ned Cort
#1 FRENCH ENTRAPMENT   (C30-018, $1.95)
#2 ALPINE GAMBIT   (C30-019, $1.95)

To order, use the coupon below. If you prefer to use your own stationery, please include complete title as well as book number and price. Allow 4 weeks for delivery.

WARNER BOOKS
P.O. Box 690
New York, N.Y. 10019

Please send me the books I have checked. I enclose a check or money order (not cash), plus 50¢ per order and 20¢ per copy to cover postage and handling.*

_____ Please send me your free mail order catalog. (If ordering only the catalog, include a large self-addressed, stamped envelope.)

Name_____

Address_____

City_____

State_____ Zip_____

*N.Y. State and California residents add applicable sales tax.